# Adam Parker and the High School Bully

By

Michael Field

This is a work of fiction. The events and characters described herein are imaginary and are not intended to refer to specific places or living persons. The opinions expressed in this manuscript are solely the opinions of the author and do not represent the opinions or thoughts of the publisher.

Up on the Roof publishing

PRINTED IN THE UNITED STATES OF AMERICA

For my children
Follow your dreams

# Chapter 1
## Play Through

Fred Thompson loved the game of golf. He just wasn't any good at it. From his drive on the first tee that found the small, scum-infested pond beyond the fairway to the 60-yard chip shot that sailed over the green and into a bunker, this morning's round was shaping up to be more of the same. Bad golf.

It was a shame that the quiet, autumn morning was marred by the sounds of golf balls smacking against trees, splashing into lakes and bouncing off cart paths. Then to be followed by a myriad of curse words. For the golfers who frequented the *Brookville Public Golf Course*, it was business as usual. Everyone knew Fred Thompson and his golf game or lack thereof. Thompson varied his playing time throughout the week, always working around his sales job. He was adept at finding gaps in his day that could be filled with a quick round of nine. But on Friday he had a permanent tee-time reservation for eighteen holes and he rarely missed it.

It was as constant as the slice in Thompson's swing and he had the wickedest of slices. Most right-handed scratch golfers suffered from this ailment. Drivers and irons were all the same for Thompson. Slice. After a ball strike, Thompson would watch his ball sail gently in the air and then slowly fade right. Away from the fairway, away from the light rough, deep into the woods and typically behind a tree. On rare occasions, he wouldn't slice at all, but rather fire, as if from a gun, the ball from the tee directly to the right. Golf shots rarely flew straight and true for Fred Thompson.

At the suggestion of his friends, Thompson even tried to play the slice. Setting up and aiming to the left of his target, hoping the ball would naturally glide to the right, as it always did and land not where he was aiming, but where he anticipated the slice would take the ball.

That's when he developed a hook.

Now, instead of having his golf shots sail to the right, Thompson developed a tendency to send the ball to his left. This opened up a Pandora's Box of bad shots and no matter how Thompson addressed the ball, whether on the tee, the fairway or the rough – and it was mostly from the rough – he never knew where the ball would go. Nothing worked to help his swing. Lessons didn't stick. YouTube videos were too confusing. Simple tips from other players fell on deaf ears.

Ultimately, Thompson gave up trying to fix his swing. He accepted his fate as a bad golfer. He liked playing. He liked walking the course, away from the distraction of the sales world. He enjoyed everything about golf. He was just never going to excel at it and he was all right with that.

The air was crisp on this particular morning. The beginning of the fall season had arrived, so early morning rounds of golf were at a premium before the weather turned too cold for any golf at all. These were the days when Thompson wrestled with the possibility of leaving Connecticut and its cold seasons for a warmer climate and golf all year round. A conversation point he frequently brought up with his wife, Susan, to no avail. Thompson secretly prayed for a long winter of snow and ice to soften his wife's staunch refusal to leave her hometown of Brookville.

The front nine was not kind to Thompson. Par score, which is the amount of shots it should take a golfer to get the ball in the hole from the tee, for the front nine was thirty-five.  Thompson's scorecard flirted with fifty, but he couldn't be too sure since he stopped keeping track of his score after hitting three straight drivers off the fifth hole tee box into the condominium complex that ran alongside the course.

Today, Thompson's group consisted of one man, Benny Jefferies, a retired bus driver, who picked up the game after getting a set of clubs as a retirement gift from the *Brookville Bus Authority*. Ten lessons and five years later, Jeffries's score always circled the course par every round he played. That was a sore spot for Thompson whenever he teamed up with Jeffries for a round of golf and this morning was no different.

Jeffries and Thompson walked the course this morning, each with their clubs in a rolling cart. Jeffries's tee shot from the 11th was dead center in the fairway. He knelt down and checked the ball's position. He cleaned grass clippings from its path, concerned it would affect his upcoming ball strike. He looked to his right, along the outskirts of fairway. Thompson stood over his ball. His tee shot had drifted right and was headed into the woods which ran the length of the fairway, leading up to the green. But when the ball went into the woods, it bounced off a rock and came back towards the fairway.

"That's some kick," Jeffries said.

Thompson smiled. "I'll take it. Me or you?"

"Go for it," Jeffries said. He waved Thompson on for his second shot.

His 8-iron already in hand, Thompson addressed the ball. He spread his feet, leaving the ball, in relation to his body, more towards his back foot. This allowed him to gain lift on the ball when he swung through or so the 15-year-old golf prodigy from a YouTube video claimed it would do.

He tightened his grip on the club's rubber handle. He waggled. He shifted. He flexed his shoulders. It didn't look like it, but this was Thompson's routine. He took a deep breath and swung.

"Shit!"

The ball fired from its place on the grass and sailed directly into the woods. Thompson dropped his head. A familiar sight.

"Take a drop?" Jeffries asked.

"Let me take a look first. Could get lucky." He slammed his club back in the bag. He made the familiar trek into the woods. He didn't hang around to see Jeffries's second shot drop on the green, two feet from the cup.

Thompson's search for the errant shot took an immediate disgusting turn as he stepped in a pile of deer droppings. Little beads of feces, no bigger than a thumbnail, piled high. "God Dammit." Thompson wiped his golf shoes on a patch of dirt, hoping to rub off the mess.

Once satisfied he had successfully cleaned the bottom of his shoes, he kicked around the underbrush of the woods, hoping to reveal his ball's position or even find another golfer's lost shot. He brought his gaze up from the ground; deeper into the woods. Something moved. A patch of yellow that walked towards him. Instantly Thompson returned his glance down, not recognizing what he had seen. Once his brain registered the yellow was a sweater, he looked up and realized he wasn't alone in the woods.

It was another golfer, wearing a yellow sweater and tan khakis. Not an uncommon site on the course. Attire that fit the sport. The golfer draped a 3-iron over his shoulder. He smiled and waved at Thompson, who returned the gesture. Thompson sensed something about the man. He was familiar, but he couldn't place the face.

"Hello. You haven't seen my ball, have you?" The golfer smiled. Hair shot out from under a plain, red baseball cap. No insignia.

Thompson paused, still trying to place the golfer's face. He couldn't. "Not really. Kind of in the same mess."

"Do I know you?"

Thompson smiled. "I was just thinking the same thing. I do play an awful lot around here."

The golfer shook his head. "No. I don't think so. I feel like we met a long time ago." He stepped closer.

"College?" Thompson asked. He leaned back. Wary of the man, but not sure why.

"No. That's not it. I didn't go to college. I did go away for a few years, but higher education it was not." He laughed.

Thompson didn't join in the laughter. He smiled and took another step back. The golfer stepped forward to cover the distance that Thompson tried to create between them.

"I probably should get to looking for my ball," Thompson said.

The golfer never broke eye contact. "Don't you want to know where I went for those few years?"

Thompson's smile faded. "It's cool, man. I'm good."

"I wasn't," he continued. "Not back then. I was pretty messed up. Had a lot of issues."

"Hey man. We all have our tough times." Thompson stepped back again. His back butted against a tree. Before he could move around it, the golfer stepped closer.

"Tough times indeed, Fred."

The color ran from his face. "Who are you?"

"Still don't remember?" He asked, then laughed. A slow, curling laugh as if the joke was one Thompson would never understand.

Thompson's only weapon against his uneasiness was anger. He used it. He grabbed the golfer by the yellow sweater and held him tight. "Listen, I don't know you. But you should get out of here before I *do* get to know you. Understand?"

"But you do know me, Fred." He jerked his hand back and then forward.

Thompson's grip loosened. His face cringed from the pain in his stomach. He looked down from the golfer's smiling face to see the 3-iron buried into his gut. The shaft pulled out. The head of the club was missing and in its place was the blade of a knife. Blood poured from Thompson's wound. Dark red. Thick. He let go of the sweater and tried to plug the leak in his gut, but his hands were no use as they were covered in blood.

The golfer smiled again as he slammed the shaft into Fred's stomach several times over. Each stab produced a cackle of laughter that filled the woods.

Thompson coughed. Blood ran from his chin, onto his shirt. A shirt that was covered in his own blood. Tears in the linen where the knife had penetrated. Blood oozed from these holes.

The golfer stepped back. Thompson slid down the tree. Legs splayed out. Arms to his side. The multiple stab wounds to his mid-section bled out, including where the shaft of the 3-iron remained inside of him. Jutting out like a stake.

The golfer knelt down. Face-to-face. He rubbed Thompson's face, smearing blood on his cheek, almost painting with it.

He spoke softly, "I know, I know. You're thinking: *How can this happen?* Right?"

Thompson said nothing. He was dying.

"It is what it is, Fred. Take comfort in knowing that I allowed you to die and nothing more. I didn't ruin your life, wreck your marriage, maim your children. I spared you that evil. Why? Because I don't blame you. Sure, you are responsible, but not completely. No, no. You see I've got a whole evil design set up for the ring-leader. The man who made my life hell."

Thompson coughed. More blood.

The golfer was excited. "I think this is it. I don't blame you for all of it, but you had to die. You were just following the crowd. Trying to fit in. Having a laugh. I get it. I do. Know that the pain you feel now will be ten-fold for your old high school buddy. He will know what it feels like to lose everything. He will know shame. He will know fear. And then, he will know death. I'm going to destroy Adam…" He stopped.

Thompson gasped once more. His eyes froze. No more breath.

"Dammit, Fred. You killed my moment. No matter. I'm still going to kill Parker. You'll just have to find out after the fact."

The golfer stood up. Took stock of his handiwork. He noticed the blood splatter on his sweater and khakis, but he wasn't concerned about hiding his crime. He breathed deeply. He listened to the sounds of the woods. He watched the lifeless eyes of Fred Thompson glass over. Decay had begun. He heard the voice of Thompson's golf buddy. It wouldn't be long before the body would be discovered, and the plan set in motion. He quickly exited the woods. He had business in Hilldale to attend to anyway.

# Chapter 2
## On the Job

Adam ducked. A glass beaker sailed over his head and smashed against the wall behind him.  Whatever was in that beaker covered the wall and instantly ignited. The wall was engulfed in flames. Shards of glass rained down on Adam as he stood in the middle of the chemistry lab. He watched the wall behind him crack and peel from the heat of the fire. The flames climbed the wall and licked the ceiling. Another beaker smashed against the wall. More flames. Pieces of glass sprayed Adam in the face, causing several scratches.

"C'mon!" He shouted. He sought out shelter, jumping over one of the long, black marble-top lab desks.

"This is my spot. Get your own!" Kevin Simpson, his best friend and crime fighting partner, shouted at him. He also shoved Adam to claim his spot.

Adam slapped him on the side of the head. "Knock it off. This is serious."

"Now it's serious? Now!" Kevin was upset. "Remember me telling you not to piss this kid off? Remember me pleading with you not to make fun of him?"

"You know I don't listen to you."

"I hate you."

Another crash. The wall of fire roared in excitement. That seemed to squash their disagreement.

"Get in line." Adam smirked. He had a tendency rile those around him. Friends included.

Kevin ignored him. He spun his portly frame around to face their attacker. He peeked over the desktop and caught sight of the college student pacing. Pools of white covered the corners of his mouth. Kevin took note as he popped back down behind the desk.

"He looks out of his mind."

"We knew he was a bit off," Adam remarked.

"No, I mean. He's foaming at the mouth. Literally. He's gone insane."

"Maybe he's on bath salts."

Kevin paused. A new fear set in. "Don't say that. Why would you say that? Dammit. He's going to eat our faces. I know it. He's going to kill us and eat our faces."

"People on bath salts do tend to do that sort of thing, yeah."

"Why would you say that now?" Kevin asked. He clutched at his chest. "My heart. It's racing. This is it. I'm having a heart attack. It's happening."

"Can you wait until we get out of this mess?"

Adam took his turn to catch a glimpse of the now rabid, possibly high on bath salts college student. He was still pacing and slapping himself in the face with his hands. Clearly, out of his mind and out of control. The student's name was Gregory Bond. He was a suspect in the death of one of his professors. The professor was found in his office, impaled on the wall with a flagpole, the stars and stripes stained in his blood.

It took some time for Adam to solve the case, since the murder occurred during his last case of a boy scout gone mad. At the time, Adam suspected the professor's death to be connected to the Scout, as he was known now by the media. The Scout attempted to blow up a hotel out of a twisted hatred for the movie, *The Last Boy Scout*. The hotel was host to a movie convention called *Act-Con* which honored action movies. This was the brain child of Kevin, who was a movie buff when he wasn't solving crime. The convention was the first and last of its kind after the incident. Adam figured the Scout would be the zenith of scary bad guys when he restarted his small-town detective agency, but having to dodge beakers being tossed by a college student who may be on bath salts clearly corrected that assumption.

When they first arrived on campus early in the evening, they looked for Bond at his dorm room. His roommate, who finally admitted to Adam his suspicions about Bond, claimed their new lead liked to study in the science wing. Alone.

After scouring the entire building, they found Bond in one of the chemistry labs. Books covered the countertop he was sitting behind. Various finals projects piled on the counters by the windows. Beakers full of chemicals. They knew he was headed back home today after his final exam. Home being over 3,000 miles away, so this was their last chance to get an audience with him.

\* \* \*

Bond's major was Anatomy. That was Adam's first clue to suspect him as the killer. The roommate revealing his suspicions was just confirmation after weeks of surveillance on Bond and his movements. Adam and his team interviewed numerous people on campus, slowly gaining a picture on the person known as Gregory Bond. But it was the flagpole that bothered Adam the most. The way it impaled its victim, Professor Caulfield. It was too precise. One stroke through the rib cage, missing major arteries and organs, then sticking firmly into the sheetrock.

Adam thought the blow was meant to provide maximum pain before an eventual slow death. He figured someone with extensive knowledge of the human anatomy would know how to inflict that much pain, especially if the end goal was for Caulfield to suffer.

No one liked Professor Caulfield. He was no-nonsense. He didn't make time for those he deemed less intelligent than himself and he wasn't afraid to show people up, especially students. All the students that Adam interviewed offered the same sentiment: *Sorry to see him go, but he wasn't a very nice guy.*

Adam knew of the professor's caustic attitude firsthand when he met Caulfield while working the Scout case. The professor helped discover the Scout's eventual plan to build a homemade atom bomb. Smoke detectors were stolen in a series of robberies, as the Scout was looking to accumulate a large quantity of Americium-241, an isotope, for his bomb. Adam didn't mind the professor's smugness when he revealed the origin of Americium-241. Caulfield thought he was better than everyone and Adam didn't care. He was trying to solve a case. Kevin, on the other hand, did care. He was not a fan of Caulfield. Throughout their search for the professor's killer, Kevin would always bring up their first meeting and how Caulfield 'irked' him. Then again, a lot of stuff irked Kevin, so Adam paid his observational complaint no mind.

"Gregory Bond?" Adam asked, shutting the Chemistry Lab door behind him. Kevin had entered first and leaned against the wall. He always let Adam take the lead.

"Yeah," Bond didn't turn around. He kept his head down and read from his text book.

"Your final is in an hour. I hear studying this late in the game really won't improve much."

"Who said I was studying?"

"You've got the book out. Pencil. Notebook. The girl who told us where you were said and a I quote…"

"No…" Kevin whispered. Pleading Adam to not bully him.

"That *creep* is in the lab studying," Adam said, not listening nor caring about Kevin's warning.

Bond's head tilted up.

"Here's what we know and feel free to correct me if I leave anything out. Professor Caulfield was found murdered in his office. That same night, several people see you exiting the science building. Rushed. Sweaty. One witness swears they heard you muttering something about grades. That got me curious, so I pulled your transcript."

"You can't do that." Bond still had his back to them.

"You're right," Adam said with a smile, "I can't. I pulled it from the computer system with the help of a hacker friend of ours. Great girl. Kevin loves her."

"No, I don't," added Kevin.

"The point is that we got your grades. Not bad. All A's.... Except not."

"The B Minus."

"The B Minus," Adam agreed. "Intro to Physics. Professor Caulfield."

Bond's head shook back and forth. "I told him. I don't get B's. Never. There had to be some kind of extra credit I could do to bring it up. Everyone offers extra credit. But not Caulfield. No, he doesn't believe in it. Says it hides those deficient in the sciences and he couldn't allow that. Ha! Me? Deficient."

"Maybe not in science, but mental capacity? I could see that."

Bond spun around. His face red with blood. His forehead was marked up from where he was repeatedly stabbing himself with his pencil. Blood and sweat ran down his face, staining the top of his T-shirt."

"I don't think he was studying," Kevin said quietly to Adam.

"Finish your story," Bond said.

"You went to see Caulfield that night," Adam continued.

"Yes."

"You asked for extra credit again."

"No. I begged for it. I got on my knees and begged for anything to bring my grade up."

"He refused."

"He laughed!" Bond stood up. "He called me pathetic. He mocked me. He ordered me out of his office. But I wouldn't go."

"He went to his desk to call security, but he never finished dialing. You attacked," Adam said.

"I threw him to the ground. No more laughing. No more mocking. I rained down on him with my fists. The first few blows hurt. My hands ached, but then they got numb like they were made for what I was doing. Like, I was meant to end that smug prick's existence. Then it was his turn to beg. Beg for his life."

"But you didn't listen."

"I listened. I just didn't care."

"So, you impaled him. All for a B minus."

"Yes."

"How long ago did you go nuts?"

"Dude!" Kevin said.

Bond grabbed one of the beakers from the tables and hurled it towards them. The beaker smashed on the marble tabletop in front of them, its contents spilling out. Before Adam could wisecrack about the missed toss, Bond tossed a lit lighter at the spilled mess and instantly the desk was in flames.

They took cover behind the flaming desk as the beakers started smashing against the wall, exploding all on their own.

* * *

The fire had since burned out on top of the desk, which allowed Adam to catch a glimpse of a dark blob headed his way. It smacked him in the forehead, knocking him on his back. He grabbed his head, a fresh cut opened up above his eye.

"He's moved onto text books." Adam rubbed his forehead, smearing blood across it.

Biology textbooks slapped into the wall.

"We have to do something," Kevin said, still hiding behind the desk.

"Call the cops?"

"We can't do that if we die in this room."

Adam pushed himself up from the floor. He leaned against the lab desk, next to Kevin. "I'm all ears then."

"I don't know!" Kevin shouted.

Bond laughed. Loud. He kept repeating the same routine. He'd pace back and forth, grab a textbook from a stack alongside the professor's table and hurl it as his new enemies. He didn't bother to look where he was throwing.

Adam peeked again. He watched Bond's insane pattern. "I really think he's on bath salts," Adam said.

"Stop saying that!" Kevin yelled.

Bond stopped. "I can hear you, fat man. I can *smell* you."

"Why does everyone always have to go to the weight?" Kevin asked.

Adam continued to study Bond. He noticed a shadow at the doorway to the classroom. He had an idea. "What do fat men smell like, Greg?"

"You're some kind of asshole, you know that?" Kevin shoved him in the back.

Adam turned to him, "We have to keep him talking."

"About me?"

"About anything!" Adam grabbed him by the shoulder. He yanked him up, to see above the tabletop. He pointed to the door to the lab. It opened.

Kevin realized what the plan was now. He called out to Bond, who tossed another textbook. "Yeah, what do I smell like?"

Bond obliged, "Like grease. Bacon. Sausage." He took a giant sniff and sighed, "The juice of red meat is intoxicating. You must taste delicious."

"Don't eat my face!" Kevin shouted.

"Greg. Did you stop by Bath & Body before coming to school today?" Adam asked.

Before Bond could answer, someone tapped him on the shoulder. He whipped around, swinging his hand and the textbook he held with it. It connected.

"Fuck!" Becky Clarkson covered her eye. She glared at Bond with the other, good eye. "You hit me."

Bond stood still. He hit a girl. He suddenly remembered all the times his mother scolded him for hitting his sisters. It was just a moment. A lapse in his insanity. He almost apologized.

Becky delivered a right cross to his jaw. She felt the bone crack under the pressure. He screamed in pain but remained standing. She brought her right foot up and between his legs. His scream was a lot less deep this time around. He buckled, hunched over from the slow, creeping pain in his groin. Becky dealt the final blow, a right upper cut that further damaged Bond's jaw and sent him sailing back onto the floor. Knocked out cold.

"Is it over?" Kevin called out.

"It is for him," Becky replied. She rubbed her eye. It already swelled.

# Chapter 3
## Marital Problems

The campus quad was abuzz with activity, more than the usual Friday night faire. Police cars with their lights flashing. School officials shouting out instructions to their students. Fire trucks parked at various angles, hoses stretched across the quad towards the science building, Jensen Hall. The fire that began in the Chemistry Lab migrated to a large portion of the building. Most of the students on campus were located behind the yellow taped barriers watching their school ablaze. A few openly questioned with hope whether classes would resume on Monday.

It took the fire fighters an hour to get the fire under control. Much of Jensen Hall smoldered, while smaller sections remained on fire. It was going to take a crew of men to walk the inside of the building to put out the fires.

The police maintained the scene on the ground level. Their main job was keeping the students at bay to prevent anything foolish like selfies with the burning building. But, of course, that's asking the impossible.

One student broke through the yellow tape. He roamed the quad looking for someone to talk to and found Adam. "Were you inside when it was on fire?"

"Yeah. So." Adam sat in the back of an ambulance. Blanket draped over his shoulders.

The student adjusted his horned-rimmed, glasses, which had fogged up from the sweat on his face. Adrenaline pumped throughout his body, causing his hand to shake as he showed his phone to Adam. "Can I get a selfie?"

Before Adam could answer, an officer stepped in and shoved the student away adding a deep-throated threat of arrest for good measure.

Adam watched while the student was escorted back behind the yellow tape. He then turned his attention to the back of a police cruiser where Gregory Bond sat. His head bobbed while buried in his hands. He was crying. The tears of a broken man. Emotionally spent. Not an hour ago, this same kid was laughing hysterically like a comic book villain while trying to kill Adam and Kevin. And now he was crying. It didn't make sense to Adam.

Kevin appeared around the corner of the ambulance. "What are you looking at?"

"Bond. Crying."

"Seriously? Where?" Kevin was excited.

Adam pointed out the cruiser. Kevin watched with glee. "This doesn't make me as happy as it should."

"Me neither," agreed Adam. "A psychotic break, maybe?"

"He was a smart kid who put an enormous amount of pressure on himself to get good grades. He just cracked from that pressure."

"What about taking stock in being a smart kid?"

Kevin shook his head. "Being smart and being confident are two different things. Plus, if he was smart than he was probably bullied."

"You think? Not everyone is bullied."

"Spoken like a person who wasn't bullied. You forget Adam. We stopped hanging out in high school. You have no idea what life was like back then for me." Kevin let that thought hang. High school wasn't an often-talked about subject between the two friends.

Adam didn't have a reply. Both friends kept the awkward silence between them until it was broken by the familiar voice of Chief Ronald Kenney.

"Parker! Where are you?"

"That didn't take long," Kevin said.

Kenney appeared in the midst of a crowd of onlookers. He pushed through and ducked under the yellow tape without any of his men trying to stop him. They knew better. He spotted Adam and Kevin and charged right for them.

"You burned down the school?" Kenney asked.

"To be fair, we didn't start the fire," Adam said.

Kevin added, "It was always burning since…"

Kenney cut him off, "Don't finish that lyric unless you want to spend the night in jail."

Kevin bowed his head.

Adam said, "This isn't our fault, Kenney. We were simply looking to question a suspect in the death of Professor Caulfield."

"The Bond kid?"

Adam paused. "Yeah. How'd you know?"

"This may come as a shock to you, Parker. But we, the police, do know what we're doing. Pretty sure, my detectives were picking him up tomorrow."

"He's right over there." Kevin pointed to Bond in the back of the police cruiser. Still crying.

Kenney turned to see Bond in the car. He did a double-take when he noticed the kid's emotions. "That's a lot of emotion."

"We think he's troubled," Kevin offered.

Kenney looked to him. "No shit, Simpson. He murdered someone." He turned to Adam, "And why were you even investigating Caulfield's death? What'd I tell you about that?"

"I know. But… I just felt responsible."

"From the outset, I told you Caulfield had nothing to do with the Scout business. It was a coincidence. That should've been the end of it. You running around town, sticking your nose where it doesn't belong is going to get you arrested. I mean that."

"I thought you were going to say, get him killed," Kevin said.

"That, too." Kenney added.

From across the sea of onlookers, Becky ran towards them. She left her blanket on the grass as she had no need for it. Her eye was worse. Puffy and black and blue. Her cornea was red from the broken blood vessels. Bond really got her good.

"What're you talking about? Am I missing something good?" She asked.

"They already knew about Bond. The police. He was going to be arrested tomorrow," Kevin said.

"So, tonight was unnecessary?" She asked.

"Everything you three do usually is," Kenney added.

"Dammit, Adam." Becky shoved him in the chest. "We almost got killed."

"*We* almost did," Kevin said, motioning to himself and Adam. "You were fine."

"You don't look fine." Kenney reached out his hand to inspect the bruise, then decided against it. It looked painful. "The EMTs check out that eye?"

"It's just a shiner."

"A shiner?" This came from behind Kenney. Mark Clarkson. He was still wearing his work suit, sans tie, and he was not pleased with the sight of his wife and her three friends.

"Mark. Why are you here?" Becky asked.

"I got a call from the cops saying that you were involved in an attack and... What the hell?" He noticed the black eye. "Are you serious? What happened?"

"Mr. Clarkson, from what I gather, your wife stopped a murderer from adding these two morons to his ledger." Kenney jabbed his thumb towards Adam and Kevin.

"This is unbelievable," Mark said.

"She was pretty great, Mark." Adam said.

Mark stared at him. He said nothing. He held the gaze until Adam bowed his head. The bad blood between them was nothing new. Mark turned to Becky. "Can we talk please?" He ushered her away from the crowd, but not far enough away to go unheard.

Kenney laughed. "Oh boy, Parker. He does *not* like you."

"I'm sure you two can form a club," Adam added.

Becky wrestled free from her husband's grasp. "What's your problem?"

"You know what it is. Ever since your friend came back to town, you've been out almost every night doing who knows what. You come back with cuts and bruises. And now, look at your eye!"

"It's just a black eye. It didn't even hurt."

"Who are you? Where is my wife?"

"This is who I am."

"No. It's not. This is someone having a mental breakdown."

"Did you ever think that maybe the person you married was living a life she didn't like?"

"Your kids. Our marriage. You don't like them."

"You know that's not what I meant. I love you. I love our children. I love everything we've done, but that's just it. It's ours. This. Tonight. All those nights. That's me. That's what I love. If you love me, then you should understand that I care about this."

"You're being selfish."

"What about your fantasy football? The bowling league. I don't like either of those things, but I know you do. I don't judge you for them."

"You're comparing risking your life on a nightly basis with me spending a night drinking beer and hanging out with friends."

"These are my friends!"

"I don't care!"

The crowd, aware of the domestic dispute occurring in front of them, stuck their smart phones in the air for better angles.

Becky started, "Look…"

"No," he cut her off. "You're doing things at the expense of our family. You were supposed to drive Caitlyn to her basketball game last week, but what happened? You were too busy on stakeout with your friends. I took her. Jake needed new cleats for soccer."

"I got those."

"You got the wrong size. His shoe size grew, and he told you this, but you fly on autopilot half the time. Never listening to any of us."

Becky stopped. She leaned back. Hands on hips.

"What are you saying?"

"I just want my wife back. The kids want their mother back."

"I love my kids. I love you. But Mark. Go fuck yourself. And if you don't understand why I said that, then you have no idea who the fuck you married. Now get home and make sure the kids get to bed tonight. I'll be back late. If you want to continue this discussion on how much of a shitty parent and wife you think I'm being and how it's such a big inconvenience to your life by all means, wait up. I'd love to keep hearing it."

She walked away with no thought of looking back. Mark kicked the dirt and stormed off. The smart phones powered down. The fight was over.

Adam, Kevin and Kenney remained still. Agog. They heard it all.

Becky wasn't in the mood to joke. "Are we done here?"

She charged into the night towards her mini-van, which had become the Parker Agency vehicle, parked along the side of the street. Adam shrugged his shoulders and followed. Kevin looked to a stunned Kenney.

"She's my ride."

He raced after them.

# Chapter 4
## Strained Relationship

The next day, news about the student, rumored to be high on bath salts, murdering his professor over bad grades was blasted all over the local morning news shows. The talk then moved to the fire, that ensued in the capture of the student, that caused considerable damage to Jensen Hall and thrusted the campus of *Connecticut State University* into chaos, especially for the science majors. There were interviews with students and other professors. Janitors that worked the science wing offered their theories on where the student could've picked up bath salts. Everything about the Gregory Bond's capture was known by the people of Hilldale and its neighboring towns. Everything except Adam and the Parker Detective Agency.

Kevin knew that Adam didn't care either way. Credit or not, he was biding his time. At least that's what Kevin assumed. Even though Adam returned to Hilldale over four months ago and began taking new cases, there was always a feeling in the pit of Kevin's stomach that Adam would leave if something better came along. After high school, Adam spent years trying to figure out what he wanted to do with his life.

But Kevin already knew Adam was meant to be a detective. It was in his blood. So, while Adam bounced from job to job, ultimately settling on a failed attempt to be an actor, Kevin never gave up hope that one day Adam would return to Hilldale. But when he returned, Adam was a broken man, distraught over the loss of his girlfriend and mired in a depression centered on his lot in life. He turned to Kevin for guidance.

It was a case that helped shine the light on Adam's true calling. The robbery of Kevin's father's hardware store proved to be just what Adam needed as they ultimately discovered the Scout and his plans for Hilldale domination.

Since they captured the Scout, Kevin sensed Adam's interest waning. He knew the signs before, as it was right after they graduated high school that Adam left Hilldale. High school was a different time for Kevin and Adam. Throughout their childhood days, the two friends were inseparable. Solving crimes all day and watching movies most nights. Once high school started, everything changed. Kevin wasn't popular, and Adam wanted to be. It's an unoriginal tale of growing up. Friends grow apart. It happens. A lot. It was a long time ago, but the past distance in their relationship permeated Kevin's thoughts when it came to the future of their detective agency.

Kevin loved being a detective. He wanted to grow up in Hilldale, solve crimes and get paid while doing it. For that to happen, they needed press. People needed to know what they could do. Adam was always reluctant to seek credit or gain fame. He was always fighting the joy that solving crimes provided and Kevin knew why.

Adam wasn't native to Hilldale. He moved to the small, Connecticut town when he was eight-years-old. He was born in New York City, where his father was an NYPD detective. Kevin didn't know the details, only that Adam's father was killed in the line of duty and his mother moved to Hilldale to raise Adam. When they were kids, Adam talked about his Dad very sparingly, but when he did, Kevin knew his father was well-known. Adam's mother would always tell the both of them that she was reminded of his father every time she saw them running around solving crimes. Granted, these were mostly cases of missing homework or stolen toys, but Kevin got the sense that Adam inherited his gift from his father. And for whatever reason, he resisted it.

They became instant friends during that first week when Adam moved to Hilldale. They solved a missing apple pie case the second week and opened the agency on the third week. They were meant to be. Becky joined them in their adventures a few months later and the team was whole.

Kevin walked across the street, from his parent's house. He still lived at home, but these days it was a necessity to save money. Plus, Adam didn't want to move out and get an apartment. In fact, all three members of the agency lived in the same houses where they grew up. Adam returned home, while his mother currently lived in Florida. With Adam all across the country, trying to find himself, his mother decided to move some place where she didn't have shovel snow anymore. The house was all paid up. All Adam needed to do was take care of utilities.

Becky bought her old house after her father passed away. Her mother moved to a retirement village where she enjoyed a variety of activities and no longer needed to worry about the basement flooding. That was Becky's concern now. Kevin's house was across the street from both of them. It was a triangle of detectives.

As Kevin knocked on Becky's front door, he thought it was weird that none of them ever moved away from home. Before that thought depressed him even more, the front door swung open. Becky stood there. Her eye swollen to the size of a super-ball.

"Why do they keep saying he was on bath salts?" Kevin referenced the news shows.

"Can we do this tomorrow?" Becky asked.

"I don't want to do it now, but if I don't return the equipment we borrowed, Nancy is going to murder me."

"Stop."

"I'm serious. I'm pretty sure I saw some drawings of various ways to kill a man at her house."

"Stay at her house often, do you?" She prodded.

Kevin stuttered. "Just when we're working on a case."

She laughed. "We both know you've gone on a few dates with her."

"Purely for a case." Kevin wasn't ready for the ridicule. "We're not a couple."

"Does she know that?"

"Can we just go?"

Becky laughed. "You can't fool me, Kevin Simpson. You like her."

"Hey!" Adam walked over from his front yard. He crossed the usual path from his house to Becky's font door. There was a matted-down dead patch of grass to confirm this.

"Please don't tell Adam," Kevin rushed in saying.

"He already knows."

"What? No."

"No what?" Adam asked. He hopped on the first step.

Kevin waved off the question. "I don't want to take the stuff to Nancy's house today, but Becky insists we do it."

"But without me," she added. "I can barely see out of this eye, plus I have some marriage repairing to do with Mark."

"I don't think your husband likes me," Adam said.

"Get in line." Becky smiled. "The mini-van is open. Grab the stuff and take it to Nancy's."

As Becky waved good-bye, shutting the front door, Adam turned to Kevin. "You going to be okay?"

"With what? I can carry the equipment."

"Seeing Nancy with me there? Will it be awkward. Are you kissing hello yet?"

Kevin whined. "Please stop."

"What? I'm curious."

"No, you're bothering me."

The bickering continued through the unloading of the mini-van and packing up of Kevin's car. It mellowed out on the drive over, but the lingering threat of Adam's teasing made Kevin uneasy.

Adam broke the silence. "You see the news?"

"The bath salts? Why do they keep bringing that up?"

"Not the bath salts," Adam said.

"The fire?" Kevin asked.

"No."

"Was it how the cops stopped a bad guy with no help from anyone else?"

"Again with that?" Adam countered.

"It would be nice though. To actually get noticed for the good work we do."

"Good work? We photograph cheating spouses most of the time."

Kevin shook his head. He turned the wheel and the car went right. "We stopped a bomb from exploding this summer. Last night was big. We solved a murder."

"Those are just two cases of many. That's it."

"Two huge cases," Kevin took a breath, "My point is that if we want to get more business and get paid, people need to know we're doing some good."

Adam stopped talking. He looked out the window. This fight was a month old. Kevin wanted press. Adam doesn't know what he wants. He turned his attention to the radio until something familiar came on. A song from the 90s about teen angst. The usual.

They unpacked half of Kevin's beat-up Sorrento when Nancy Olliver appeared in her doorway. Camouflage pajamas, top and bottoms. She held a steaming cup of coffee in her hands, which she brought to her mouth for a sip while she watched Kevin took a milk crate full of equipment from his trunk and placed it on the driveway.

He waved with his free hand. She smiled.

Adam placed another crate on the driveway and leaned in closer to Kevin, who was rummaging through a milk crate of wires and computer cables. "No kiss. Interesting."

"Leave me alone," Kevin whispered back.

"You're being a baby." Adam returned to the car for a computer monitor.

Kevin stacked a box onto the milk crate. He picked both up and walked towards Nancy.

"I see you caught your man," Nancy said.

"Yup," he nodded. "Your stuff really helped us out."

"I don't know why you just didn't let me come with you."

"I told you. Adam likes to keep the team small."

Nancy scoffed. "And I told you. I don't believe you. I think you don't want me there."

"That's... No. That's not true," he stammered.

Nancy walked down her front steps. Closer to Kevin. "Look. At some point, you're going to have to tell them that me and you are together."

Kevin shot a glance at Adam, who was reaching into the Sorrento's trunk looking for more wires, no doubt. "I don't want to. Besides, he already knows that something is up. And he's just started teasing me. If I tell him we're steady..."

"No one says *steady* anymore, Kevin," She cut him off.

"Regardless, he'll be all over me about you. I can't take it."

"I can beat him up for you if you'd like."

"Yeah, that's not an option."

"Keeping secrets isn't either."

He drew a big breath. "I know. And together? We've been out a few times. Watched some movies. It's not like we're..."

"Don't say steady," she smiled.

"Then what are we?" he asked.

Nancy smiled again. "I know we live in the age of the casual hook-up, but I'm not that type of girl, Kevin Simpson." She shoved her finger in Kevin's chest. "And after what we did the other night, I'd say we're definitely more than the 1950s version of steady."

Kevin gulped. "That's a fair point."

"I mean, you cried..."

"Who cried?" Adam asked as he dropped a crate of wires at Nancy's feet.

Kevin jumped. "No one. Someone lied, but not cried. You heard it wrong. I'm going to take this stuff into the house." He piled a milk crate and another box onto Adam's box, then lifted all three in an effort to avoid furthering the conversation.

"You don't want help?" Adam asked.

"Nope," he grunted. Kevin struggled as he climbed the stairs. Each step shakier than the last. Nancy was quick to open the door for him as he charged through doorway and ended in an audible crash.

"I can't look," Nancy said.

"I'm sure it's fine," Adam offered.

Glass and plastic crunched from inside. "I'm pretty sure this stuff was broken before I came in here," Kevin lied.

Nancy dropped her head. "Son of a..."

"So," Adam cut her off. "How have you been?"

"What do you want?" Nancy wasn't in the mood.

Kevin appeared in the doorway. "Yeah, what're you doing?"

"Nothing. I was making conversation," protested Adam.

"I've been fine, Adam. Thanks for asking."

"Great. See, Kevin. Just talking. I wasn't going to say anything to embarrass you like the fact that I know you've been seeing each other for a few weeks now." Adam smiled.

"Shit," Kevin said. "C'mon, Adam. Enough."

"And how'd you figure that out?" Nancy asked.

"A good detective never reveals..."

"He followed me," interrupted Kevin.

Adam nodded. "I followed him."

"He's your friend. Why would you follow him?" Nancy stepped closer to Adam.

"Because I was concerned about him. That's what friends do for one another."

"No. Friends ask their friends about their life. They show genuine interest. They don't stake them out hoping to find dirt on them."

"I wasn't looking for dirt." Adam was defensive.

So was Nancy, "Maybe you should ask yourself why Kevin decided to keep the two of us being together from you. Why would he not want you to know that he's seeing me?"

"Or maybe I should ask him that?" Adam shot back.

"Go ahead." Nancy called his bluff.

They both turned to Kevin, who was doing his best to extradite himself from the conversation. It failed. He wanted no part of it. "Can we go? Nancy, I'll call you later."

Kevin dropped his head to avoid eye contact and made a straight line for the car. Adam's smile widened.

Nancy glared at him. Emotionless. "I'm not a big fan of you, Parker. I tolerate you because Kevin looks up to you and I'm a big fan of him. But one day, he won't be. One day, your behavior is going to force Kevin to make a decision and you might not like it."

"Jesus. What does that mean?"

She pointed her finger in his face. "Just be careful or you might end up like your old high school pal, Fred Thompson."

"What happened to Fred?"

Nancy left Adam on the front walk. She returned to her home, shutting the front door behind her without even a wave *goodbye*. Adam remained still. He looked to Kevin, who had already started the car.

"Kevin. Google Fred Thompson."

# Chapter 5
# Old Friend

*Crepes and Coffee* was a new café that popped up in downtown Hilldale over a year ago. Fancier than the *Hilldale* Diner, the usual breakfast spot for most residents, and far more expensive. The high prices didn't stop the droves of people from experiencing fancy French pastries and over-priced macchiato drinks.

Kevin was annoyed, which meant he was hungry. Adam preferred *Crepes and Coffee* over the diner. He couldn't stand another greasy egg sandwich with a side of lukewarm home fries, a *Hilldale Diner* special.

They sat at a table by the window looking out over Main Street. It was early, so most of the shops and restaurants that lined this particular area of downtown were yet to open. Adam found himself staring at the large plastic shrimp attached to the top of the *Slammin' Sushi* restaurant across the street. At night, the shrimp was quite the sight as it lit the entire block in a pinkish neon. When the *Slammin' Sushi* first opened, people would drive by to get a look at the giant pink shrimp in the night sky. But in the daylight, the shrimp was a dirty, pink plastic eyesore with all its flaws exposed.

Adam's gaze was locked on the giant plastic shrimp, not because he was studying it, but rather he was deep in thought. He remembered his days at *Hilldale High* and the years spent sitting at his locker with Fred Thompson. Adam and Fred had the misfortune of being dropped off at school earlier than most kids. Adam's mother's job required her to be in an hour before school started, so the only option was to drop Adam off early. Fred's father worked as a foreman for a construction outfit, which meant he was often needed on job sites before the crew showed.

They met the first week of freshman year. They sat on the floor, their lockers at their back and talked, ate breakfast and had a few laughs. Adam smiled, remembering all the jokes they told and stories they shared. He was the first friend he made at *Hilldale High* and for that reason, among others, he counted Fred as one of his best friends.

"Nothing goes into detail. All the stories just say he was killed under suspicious circumstances while he was playing golf." Kevin had his phone on the table. With one hand, he slid his finger up on the screen to scroll the article while his other hand stabbed at a blueberry stuffed crepe with a fork.

"He was murdered, then?" Adam asked. Eyes still locked on that plastic shrimp.

"Is that what suspicious circumstances mean?" He shoved a forkful of crepe into his mouth. Blueberry sauce dripped down his chin.

"I think so." Adam sipped from the cup of coffee on the table. He grimaced. "This is cold."

"Well, you've been staring out the window for the last ten minutes. What'd you expect?"

"Nothing, I guess."

Kevin put his fork down. "How close were you and Fred?"

"I hadn't seen him in a while, but we kept in touch. *Facebook*, texting, that sort of stuff. I was in his wedding party, but that was years ago. I can't believe someone would murder him."

"We just fended off a crazed college student over a B-minus. I can believe anything."

"Do you remember Fred from school?" Adam asked.

"Yeah, I do," Kevin said, purposely not wanting to go into detail.

"He was so funny. We'd crack jokes constantly every morning before school began. We both got dropped of early, so we'd just sit at our lockers. Eating breakfast and having fun."

"Sounds like a good friend."

"He is. He was." Adam didn't like having to correct himself. "Well, dammit... I wish we hadn't lost touch."

"People move on. Friends change. You and I both know that," Kevin pointed out the window. "The sushi restaurant you've been staring at. You know who works there?"

Adam shrugged. He sipped his coffee again, forgetting it was cold. "Why'd I do that?" He put the cup down and shoved it across the table.

"Jeff Tanaka."

"Tanaka-Bomb?"

Kevin smiled out of deference. "The very same. He came back to Hilldale a month or so ago after training somewhere as a chef. That restaurant is his uncle's business. He's been head chef ever since he got back."

"Wasn't he a huge nerd in high school?"

"So was I. My point is that he was never known for cooking. He was into video games and horror movies. But people grow up. They change. I changed. You changed. I think."

"I changed," Adam declared.

"You've gotten older," countered Kevin.

"Is this about Nancy? I was trying to help you."

"In what way? Spying on me to find dirt to make fun of me with?"

Adam paused. He leaned back. Not having an answer for Kevin. He grabbed his coffee cup and held it up for someone behind the counter to see. He mouthed 'more coffee' and returned to see Kevin's unimpressed face.

"I don't know how I was trying to help you. All right?" Adam admitted.

"It's not all right. You shouldn't be following me. I can have a private life."

"I know, but you were acting weird. Purposely not telling me your plans, so I got curious and followed you one night. I should've said something, but I didn't know when to bring it up that I knew about you and Nancy."

Kevin shook his head. He looked out the window. Collecting his thoughts. "I didn't tell you because I didn't want to hear you."

"What's that mean?"

"It means," Kevin paused. He was uncomfortable broaching this subject, "You tend to be mean when you think you're just teasing me."

"But I'm not laughing at you. I'm laughing with you."

"But I'm not laughing."

"Well, that's more of a not-having-a-sense-of-humor problem."

"You're doing it again," Kevin countered.

Adam threw up his hands. "I can't win."

Kevin stood up. He tossed a few bills on the table. "Let's just drop it. We got other things to do. Fred's funeral is today. We should go."

"I know." Adam agreed. "I just don't want to."

"No one ever wants to go to these things."

* * *

The funeral was in Brookville. Fred married a girl who lived in the town, so it was understood that Fred would leave Hilldale to start his married life in the small inland town that is known for its fair share of strange occurrences. The murder of a golfer was not as shocking as four missing teens in a corn maze one Halloween season years ago. That case was unsolved, and Kevin still talked about it as they left the car and walked across the cemetery to the congregation of mourners around an open plot.

"Never heard from again?" Adam asked.

"That's what they say. If we've got time, we should stop by the local sheriff station and ask if we could see the file." Kevin's tone revealed his excitement at the prospect of diving into a possible supernatural case.

"Number One. No. Number Two. They'd kick us out. Honestly, I don't know how Kenney puts up with us half the time."

"This is true," Kevin said. "But still, I've always wanted to investigate that case."

Adam stopped walking. "You remember in 8th grade? The Danny Stevenson case? We were asked to find his favorite baseball card. I know you remember."

Kevin dropped his head, "Yeah."

"We had to come to Brookville. We suspected that Danny's older brother took it when the parents split up and they moved to Brookville. You remember what we found."

Kevin nodded. "We said we wouldn't talk about that again."

"Exactly. I'm not going down that road again. I don't want to have anything to do with...strange occurrences." Adam walked on to the funeral.

"Chicken."

"You're damn right," Adam said, not bothering to turn around.

The priest finished up the ceremony just as Adam and Kevin melded with the crowd. Adam made eye contact with Fred's wife, Sharon. She wore a black dress along with a small black hat and veil. Her blonde hair poked through the netting of the veil. Her pale skin had reddened from the coolness of the autumn air. This is how Adam remembered her many years ago. Rosy cheeks, pale skin and a laugh that was infectious. She smiled at him, tears in her eyes. Adam didn't smile back. He couldn't.

There's never a good way to handle the emotions of beloved's death and Adam wasn't breaking any ground in figuring that out. While Kevin bowed his head, Adam periodically scanned the crowd, looking at the faces of the people paying their respects. All somber. All quiet. Some tears.

The crowd dispersed. Adam excused himself and apologized his way through the sea of mourners to get to Sharon. When he was close enough, he reached out and touched her arm. She turned and instantly hugged him. The strength of the hug surprised Adam.

"I found out this morning. I'm so sorry."

"He loved you so much." She reached out and stroked his cheek with her gloved hand. Her smile wouldn't fade. Adam suspected medicinal help to keep Sharon calm.

"Is there anything you need?" Adam asked.

She shook her head. "He was going to call you. Kept saying how he wanted to see you again. Especially since you came back."

"I know. I wanted to call as well, but I got caught up with a few things in Hilldale."

"We read about it. We were so proud. Fred kept saying he wanted to see you again." There was a glaze in Sharon's eyes. She was losing focus.

"I know, Sharon. I know." Adam hugged her again. She squeezed him again, stronger than before.

Another family member, seeing Sharon's look of confusion, came over and helped her to a black sedan. Adam sensed her drug-induced state had been constant for the past few days and understandably so. People handled tragedy in many different ways. There's no rule book on how to deal with it when it hits home. Just get through it.

Kevin had a tougher time getting through the people surrounding the cemetery plot. He reached Adam just as he turned from saying goodbye to Sharon. "She okay?"

"About as well as can be expected," Adam replied.

"What now?"

"We go home."

"What about offering to help? Bring the Parker Agency on board."

Adam placed his hand on Kevin's shoulder. He squeezed. "And how would that work out? Consoling someone in their time of grief, all the while looking to pick up some work."

"When you say it like that, kind of makes me look like a jerk-off for suggesting it."

"Excuse me." A voice from behind them.

They turned to see a Brookville's deputy smiling back at them. He held his hands on his hips, a common stance amongst law enforcement. "You wouldn't happen to be Adam Parker, would you?"

Kevin sighed. "Did Chief Kenney call you?"

"Who? Is he from Hilldale?"

"Yeah," Adam held out his hand and shook the deputy's hand. "What can we help you with?"

"Would you mind coming with me?" He turned and headed into the cemetery.

Kevin tugged at Adam's shirt to get his attention. "We're not even thirty minutes in this town and you're in trouble."

Adam shrugged. They followed the deputy; walking several yards to a collection of more deputies and a large man with a tight gray beard. Gray hair. Not quite thin, but not over-weight. Thick in every respect. This was Sheriff Ty Copeland.

Adam held up his hand in a small wave. "Adam Parker. What seems to be the trouble?"

Copeland stared at him before responding. "I just got off the phone with a Chief Ronald Kenney. He knows you."

"Yes. I've worked with Chief Kenney before."

"In my experience, when an officer knows someone, it's usually because that person is either a criminal or a pain in the ass."

"I assure you, it's the latter. One of his biggest."

Copeland chuckled. "He said the same thing."

Adam nodded. "Of course, he did." He looked to the deputies standing around, but they're faces betrayed zero emotion.

"Did Kenney say anything bad about us?" Kevin asked.

"Who are you?" Copeland shot back.

"Just an associate of Mr. Parker's."

"I didn't ask to see you."

Adam held up his hand. "Sheriff. What did you need for me to do?"

Copeland took a deep breath. He slow-burned from Kevin to Adam. "I need you to leave town as soon as possible."

Adam laughed. "Because of one phone call from Chief Kenney?"

"Because of this." Copeland pointed to a gravestone in front of him. Adam didn't realize they were all standing around a grave.

Adam stepped forward, toward the group of officers. He looked at the gravestone. As soon as he saw it, his mind raced. Questions flooded his brain, but only one escaped his lips. "This a joke?"

"Not the kind I like," Copeland said. "And quite frankly, not a very funny one to begin with."

Adam waved Kevin over. The gravestone was a simple rounded piece of granite. On the front was red lettering. Spray painted. The paint ran before drying, but the message was clear.

Adam Parker is next.

# Chapter 6
## The Message

As soon as they were in the car, Kevin's cell phone rang. It was Chief Kenney. He wanted them to meet him at *Lonnie's Tavern*, a dive bar located in downtown Hilldale, pretty much right around the corner from where they had breakfast at *Crepes and Coffee.* Kevin agreed, not bothering to check with Adam. His thoughts were on the threat scrawled on the gravestone back at the Brookville cemetery.

Someone killed Fred Thompson, Adam knew that much, but not what it had to do with him. Aside from the occasional phone call or *Facebook* message, he hadn't seen Thompson in years. He wanted to stay and find out what exactly the Brookville Sheriff's department knew about the case and if they had any leads, but the cold reception from Sheriff Copeland was enough to push Adam away from that idea. Instead, he opted to regroup and figure out exactly what happened to Fred and how it related to him. Once they were on the highway, Adam finally asked about the cell phone call.

"We're meeting him at *Lonnie's*," Kevin said.

"And he said he had to show us something?" Adam asked.

Kevin nodded. "He wouldn't tell me what, but right now, I'm more concerned about the threat we just walked away from."

"That wasn't a threat," Adam lied.

"Fine. The message then. Can we talk about it?"

"What's to say?"

Kevin slapped the steering wheel. "Jesus, Adam. Your friend was just murdered and now there's a note saying that you're next. I think there's plenty to talk about. Like, who killed Fred? Why'd they kill him? Why are you next? Do you and Fred have any common enemies? Who wants to kill you?"

"What do you think I've been doing for the last 20 minutes? I've been thinking about all of those questions and more. There's nothing more to say about it because I don't have any of the answers." Adam was agitated.

"Well. Then," Kevin looked for something less obvious to say. "We need to get these answers." He failed.

"We should have Becky meet us at *Lonnie's*," Adam said.

"If it doesn't ruin her marriage, sure."

"You think they're in trouble?"

"Other than being in love with Becky, the other thing that you and her husband have in common is that he doesn't like you playing detective either."

"I'm not in love with Becky."

"Whatever you want to call it, you have it for her."

"You think she's going to quit?"

"I don't know. But if she did, I'd understand. Family comes first."

"We're family, too. Right? The three of us."

Kevin shrugged. "I don't know. Are we?"

Adam motioned to say more, but he had nothing to say. He turned his head and watched the landscape of the Merritt Parkway fly by the window.

"Call her. If she can meet us, great. If not, don't push it," Kevin finally said.

* * *

Like most of Hilldale's downtown bars and restaurants, *Lonnie's Tavern* didn't have a parking lot. They relied on street parking. Kevin found a spot across the street from the bar, a rarity this time of the day. They approached the front door, when a maroon sedan pulled up behind them alongside the curb. It was Mark's car. Becky got out from the passenger seat and smiled at Adam and Kevin, before spinning around to talk to Mark. She leaned on the window. But the car drove away, leaving the conversation one sided.

Becky raised her hands in disbelief, then covered her face. Adam noticed the tear-stained cheeks and watery eyes.

"How much did you see of that?" Becky asked. Her head still in her hands, as she wiped her face clean of emotion.

"See what?" Adam asked.

"Nice try," she replied.

"So, uh, you want to talk about it?" Kevin offered.

"Not really." Becky shifted her stance.

Kevin nodded, "Yeah, I didn't think so."

"He's right. I am a crappy mom," she cut him off. "I just get so angry and defensive when he tells me the thing I'm feeling. He does it all the time. That's why I married him. He knows me better than I do."

"You're not a crappy mom," Adam said.

"You've been back for four months. How do you know?"

"Uh," he stuttered, "Kevin told me."

"Don't bring me into this." Kevin slapped Adam's arm.

Becky continued, "I don't know how much longer I can keep doing this."

"The agency?" Kevin asked.

"I love it. I really do, but I can't keep at it if it means I'm neglecting my family."

"Who says your husband can't be home and doing what it is you do?" Adam asked.

"Which is?"

"I don't know. What mothers usually do."

Kevin cleared his throat.

Becky slow-burned to Adam. If he didn't sense her rage, he was about to feel it. "You mean, like what a woman *should* be doing?"

"Yeah," Adam stopped. "No. No. No. I mean..."

Kevin clutched his friend's arm. "It's been a pleasure working with you, Adam."

*Slap!* Adam's cheek burned from the open-handed retort of Becky.

The front door opened just as Adam recoiled from the slap. Kenney caught the tail end of the slap and immediately flashed a toothy grin. Christmas came early.

"Looks like you've got another member of your fan club, Parker." Kenney held the door open. He waved them in.

Adam rubbed his cheek. He figured an apology wasn't what was needed right now, so he kept quiet and followed Becky and Kevin into the bar. Kenney was still all smiles as he held the door open.

The bar was empty sans a few regulars and a few college kids, the latter talking about the recent fire on campus and the subsequent cancellation of classes for the week. The university struggled to have classes with an entire building condemned because of fire damage.

Kevin, overhearing the conversation, turned around. "Chief, we won't get in trouble for that fire, will we?"

"Don't know. Did you start it?"

"No," Kevin said. Then got nervous. He asked Adam, "Did we?"

"No," Adam shot back.

The jukebox played a song from one of the many boy-bands that burst onto the scene during the 90s. Adam recognized the song. He spotted Kevin singing to himself and bopping his head. Kevin definitely knew it as well. They made eye contact. Kevin ceased his head bopping and hip shaking.

Becky lagged behind the group. She harbored a multitude of feelings. Remorse for the way she spoke to her husband, doubt about her current situation with the Parker Detective Agency and a bit of concern for why Kenney needed to bring them to *Lonnie's*. Smacking Adam across the face didn't weigh heavy on her mind. That didn't surprise her.

*Lonnie's* was the dump that everyone knew it to be, but it held special meaning for Becky. This was the bar where she met Mark. Home from college one summer, Becky joined her old high school classmates at *Lonnie's* to catch up on everyone's progress. Mark was a bartender back then. Earning cash over the summer to help with expenses during the fall while he studied law at *Yale University*.

About 30 minutes into learning about her high school friends' new adventures, she wanted out of the bar. She no longer had anything in common with her high school friends. This led her to the bar multiple times to get drink after drink, each time lingering a bit longer in order to talk with the cute bartender than made her laugh. Mark.

Her friends had long since left, sore over Becky's lack of interest in their lives. Becky closed the bar with Mark. He walked Becky to her car, where they shared their first kiss under the notoriously blinking street lamp that hasn't been fixed in the years since that magical night. Becky came to *Lonnie's* almost every night that Mark worked during that summer.

The memory of that summer hurt. She was angry with Mark, but also with herself. She had to decide. To choose. Her marriage or the agency. She didn't like it. It shouldn't be a choice, but it was. She had to make it.

She was quick to verbally smack down anyone that tried to control her. Actually slapping Adam, while warranted, was also not entirely because of what he said. She harbored regret over everything she'd been doing the past four months. She loved being a detective, but it was hurting everything else in her life.

Becky missed her children. The events that surrounded the Scout's plan to blow up Hilldale had filled Becky with purpose. She believed the Parker Agency was her true calling. All those years ago, running around with Adam and Kevin, solving crimes and causing trouble. Those were some of the fondest memories of her childhood. She loved it. And when Adam returned to Hilldale and immediately got involved with another case, she jumped at the chance to help out. To feel the same way, she felt all those years ago. Preventing the Scout from blowing up the hotel proved that.

But at the expense of her family? Of her marriage?

She wasn't naïve about Adam's feelings either. She knew Adam had a crush on her. She always knew. If she continued with the agency, would that crush become too much to ignore? Would Adam want more? Would *she* want more? It was a road that she didn't want to go down and yet another reason to walk away.

Kenney pushed through a group of college kids gathered at the basement door. The yellow police tape, meant to keep people away, always had the opposite effect. They peered down the stairs in hopes of catching a glimpse. Cell phones raised in the air recording something they couldn't see. As Kenney pushed through, their phones turned in his direction. He did his best to ignore the attention. He held the tape up. Adam was first down the stairs, hearing the groans from the college kids who wanted to follow.

In the basement, all that remained was the forensic team. They were in middle of processing the scene. Kenney guided the three friends through the basement until they made it to the back wall.

"Please say something. This is annoying." Adam said.

Kevin's face contorted. "What is that smell?" He got nervous. "Oh my God, if there a dead body down here? You're showing us a dead body?"

"Jesus, Simpson. Relax. I'm not showing you a dead body."

Kevin breathed easy. "Thank God."

"You're probably smelling the pile of human excrement in the corner." Kenney pointed to a sectioned off corner of the room.

Kevin's face dropped to disgust. "I think I'm going to be sick."

"That's foul, Chief." Becky added.

Kenney rubbed his neck. Not sure how to start. "Ok. Look. This is what we know. We received a phone call from one of the employees. He was in the basement, getting beer and he heard a noise. He comes over here and finds a girl. She's cowering in the corner. Trying to hide."

"He heard a noise? He didn't smell the poop first?" Kevin asked.

"The pile of human excrement was covered at that point. When we uncovered it, that's when the smell was evident," Kenney replied.

"Who is she?" Adam asked, trying to keep them on track.

"We don't know. She's at *Hilldale Hospital* right now. I'm going to be checking on her right after we're finished here," Kenney said.

"What does she have to do with Adam?" Kevin asked.

"We found something on the wall," Kenney offered.

"This have to do with Brookville?" Adam asked.

Kenney nodded.

"Brookville? What's going on?" Becky didn't like not knowing.

"You found a message, right?" Adam didn't break eye contact with Kenney. "The same one?"

"Have you been having any trouble lately?" Kenney asked.

"You're starting to freak me out," Becky said.

"Starting?" Kevin said.

"Kenney. C'mon." Adam said.

Kenney held up his hands. He stepped away from the wall and allowed Adam to take a look. Adam, Kevin and Becky all leaned towards the wall.

Carved into the stone and smeared with blood were four words.

Adam Parker is next.

\* \* \*

After seeing the message, they returned to the main floor. The forensic team continued their job in the basement. Adam nursed a beer, while Kevin sipped his watered-down soda through a straw. Kenney spoke with one of his officers, getting an update on the Jane Doe at the hospital.

Becky returned from the bathroom. She grabbed her second beer and chugged. She stifled a belch and slammed the bottle down.

"What're we going to do?" She asked.

"Adam should leave town. I'd leave town if I were him," Kevin added.

Adam studied his friends from the mirror behind the bar. They spoke to each other behind Adam, arguing about their next plan of action. Adam watched, but didn't pay attention to anything they said.

When they were kids, Adam loved being a detective. They spent all their days solving crimes. Most of the crimes were stolen comic books or missing pets, but it was a great time in Adam's life. Running around town stopping crime in its tracks. It was fun. It was exciting. Adam had a gift. He was extremely observant. He saw things others missed. It made perfect sense to play detective back then. It was in his blood, as his mother often told him. But they were kids. Once they grew up, everything changed.

When high school began, Adam wanted different things. He hated being a detective. It made him feel childish. It also reminded him of the girl who wouldn't love him back. Becky. Kevin begged to continue the agency, but Adam was done. He found new friends. New things to be passionate about.

After four years of high school ended, everyone moved apart. Adam left Hilldale, vowing to himself never to return. But fate and a bad break-up had other plans for him. He returned home with his tail between his legs, sobbing to Kevin at the *Hilldale Diner*. It was a low point Adam doesn't like to remember. After looking to regroup at his childhood home, he soon found himself embroiled in a case that ultimately led to where they were right now. Sitting a bar. Arguing about how to keep Adam alive.

All that bringing back the agency had done was have them survive several near-death experiences, Kevin was tortured by an insane middle-schooler, Becky's daughter was kidnapped, her marriage was on the rocks and Adam was currently marked for death. Not exactly the same as stopping Gordon Hedges, their arch-nemesis when they were kids, from stealing all the third graders' lunch money.

The stakes were higher now.

"Adam." Kenney sat next to him at the bar. "Anything out of the ordinary?"

"Besides the messages?" Adam replied.

"Besides that."

"No. We've been working the usual cases. There have been a few cheating spouses who didn't like that we've photographed them, but it wasn't contentious. They were just embarrassed."

"Still. Get me their names and we'll follow up," Kenny said.

"I can do that," Kevin offered. He cycled through his phone for the list.

"Chief," Becky started, "What about the girl? Who is she?"

"Still trying to figure that out. She's not talking. Just catatonic. No signs of trauma. That's her blood down there on that wall. She had a cut on her finger."

"We need to see her." Becky said.

"This is not a case," Kenney replied.

"Of course, it is. This girl wants him dead," Kevin added.

"We don't know that. We don't know anything yet," Kenney shot back.

"I also want to know what happened to Fred Thompson. How he died." Adam persisted.

"I don't think you're hearing me." Kenney spun in his stool. He faced Adam. "This isn't a case for you to investigate"

"Clearly, it's all about me. My friend is murdered. I go to the funeral and find the message on the gravestone. I come back, and the same message is in the dingy basement of some dump. There's a mystery here and it involves me. I need to solve it," Adam demanded.

"Dump? This is an *okay* bar," Becky defended her fond memories. "And we all need to find out what's happening here. Not just you. You're not alone here."

Kenney slapped his hand on the bar. A few other patrons took notice. "Let me tell you what's going to happen. As soon as you leave this bar, Adam will have 24-hour police protection." He pointed at Adam. "I will know where you are at all times. If I think you're investigating this case, I'll haul the three of you into the stationhouse and lock you up."

"You're going to arrest us?" Kevin asked.

"Parker? No. I'll keep him safe," Kenney said, "But you two, I'll arrest for obstruction."

Adam placed his hand on his chest, "I'm touched, Chief."

"Keep it up and you will be." Kenney made a fist.

Adam continued, "I have a right to find out who wants me dead"

"Sure. But I don't have to let you," Kenney held up his hands, "Look, I get it. Someone out there is gunning for me; I'm going after them. But I'm not in your situation right now. I'm in charge of keeping the town and its people safe. You included."

"So, we do nothing?" Adam asked.

"I certainly hope so," Kenney barked.

# Chapter 7
## Making Plans

Kenney kicked them out of *Lonnie's* with a promise that he'd be in touch. Not ready to leave and having no plan of action after learning about the threat on Adam's life, the three friends walked the downtown streets seeking answers to their questions. Becky hadn't eaten breakfast, so Adam again sought out his favorite breakfast spot, *Crepes and Coffee*. It was late in the morning, but Adam didn't mind a second breakfast. He had developed a crush on the coffee. He also figured it was a good place to regroup and figure out their next move. They turned the corner from *Lonnie's* and made their way towards the sweet smell of warm, pastry dough.

Becky studied the buildings. "There are a lot of empty spaces down here."

"I've been telling Adam we need to get a space," Kevin replied.

"Well, if I survive my murder, we can definitely look into it," Adam offered.

"Sorry," Kevin patted his friend on the shoulder. "So, what's the plan?"

"We need to talk with the girl. Find out who she is. Why she wants Adam dead," Becky said.

"We don't know that she wants me dead. Not yet." Adam said.

"She wrote the threat on the wall. In her own blood," Becky shot back. "That seems like a clear indication of her intentions."

Adam stopped walking. "This is about Fred. Someone killed him because of me. They knew I'd go to the funeral. They left that message on the gravestone for me."

"How could they know you'd see that particular gravestone?" Kevin asked.

"The paint was fresh. They were probably sitting somewhere in the woods that surrounded the cemetery. They waited to see if I'd arrive and then they found a gravestone that was in the direct path of everyone's car."

"That's a big guess," Becky said.

"Bigger than thinking some girl wants to kill me?"

"It was her blood!"

Adam shook his head. "It doesn't make sense. There could be a dozen couple reasons for that girl to be in the basement. She overheard someone say something about me. She read about me in the paper. She was a former girlfriend of mine."

"If she was an ex-girlfriend, why would you be next?" Kevin asked. "I mean, like next what?"

"Seriously?" Adam stared at him.

"I guess not." Kevin retreated from his question.

Adam continued "Look, Fred's death makes sense. Kill someone I was close to once. Wait for me to show. Leave me a threat."

"If someone killed Fred to get to you, wouldn't they try to kill you when you went to the funeral?" Becky asked, but kept her train of thought moving. "Better yet, why kill Fred at all? It's not like you're in hiding. If they wanted to kill you, then they can just come to Hilldale and find you."

"That's reassuring," Kevin said. "Jesus, Adam. Maybe you *should* be in hiding."

"But this is why I need to find out how and why Fred was murdered." Adam said. "I don't think it was just to lure me out to Brookville."

"That town gives me the creeps. Always has."

Becky smiled. "That's part of its charm."

"They can keep it," Kevin replied. "We also met the Brookville sheriff. He's not a fan." Kevin said.

"When has that ever stopped us before?" Adam asked.

"He's not going to let you pepper him with questions about the case."

"Then, maybe we'll have to find another way get that information," Adam suggested. He had an idea, but he knew they wouldn't like it. They never liked breaking the law.

Kevin shook his head. He already knew what Adam was thinking about doing. "You're out of your mind. No!"

"You said it yourself. He's not going to let me interview him about the case," Adam replied.

"You want to break in?" Becky was in disbelief. "Are you really saying that?"

Adam nodded. "I'm pretty sure that was obvious."

Becky pointed to a black sedan currently idling on the side of the road. "You do see that, right? That's your protection. How are you going to race up to Brookville, break into the sheriff station and get back without being noticed?"

The two plainclothes cops, inside the sedan, realized they were the topic of conversation. They waved when all three friends looked back at the sedan. They weren't trying to hide. Adam waved back.

"I didn't even see them there," Kevin said.

"They've been following us since we left the bar," Becky said.

"How did I miss that?" Kevin asked himself.

"You're not as good at this as you think you are," Becky answered.

Adam whistled. "Yikes. That was harsh."

"Thanks, Rebecca." Kevin folded his arms. He knew Becky hated being called her full name.

Becky held her hands up. "Sorry. I'm just on edge."

"Wait," Kevin jumped back to the conversation before the revelation of the Adam's protection. "You're not concerned about the potential B&E Adam is suggesting?"

"Well, I am. Sure," Becky started, "But if this was your life being threatened, wouldn't you want to know everything you could?"

"No. I'd leave town. Forever."

"I'm not doing that," Adam said.

"So, breaking into the Brookville Sheriff Station is your big plan, then?" Kevin asked, "And how are you going to do that? You're a detective. Not a professional thief."

"Details. I'll figure it out."

"You'll figure it out?" Kevin pointed his finger at Becky and himself. He wagged it back and forth. "Meaning we're not part of this."

"You think the girl is involved. You two work that angle," countered Adam.

Becky pushed through the two of them. "I'm still hungry." She headed straight for the café.

They followed. Adam continued, "We don't know what's going on yet. Someone wants me dead. But who? Why? How? The only leads we have are Fred's death and the Jane Doe in the basement. Splitting up makes sense."

"To you. It makes sense to you. Not to me. Not to Becky."

"You shouldn't go alone," Becky called back from her head start to the café.

"See."

"No. He's right, Kev," Becky added. "We have no idea what the two messages in two different locations mean. We need to investigate both of them."

"So, while me and you are somehow sneaking past a police-protected hospital room door, who's helping Adam with his B&E trip to Brookville?" Kevin asked.

Adam offered, "I don't need help."

Becky paused. She turned around. "What's your plan then? How are you getting into the station?"

Adam paused. He smiled. "My charm?"

"Call Nancy. She'll be glad to help." Becky saw no charm.

"My Nancy?" Kevin asked. He immediately knew it was a mistake. Both Adam and Becky stared at him. Smiles on their faces. "Shut-up."

Becky said to Adam, "So, it's settled. Take *his* Nancy with you to Brookville. Kevin and I will check out the Jane Doe."

"Will *his* Nancy even do this?" Adam asked.

"Dammit, I hate you guys," Kevin mumbled through a deep sigh. "And yes, she'll do it. She's been hounding me for weeks about getting more involved."

They arrived at the front door to *Crepes and Coffee*. There was nothing more to say. It was decided. Divide and conquer.

"Can we eat now?" Becky asked.

They entered the café. Their reflections growing smaller in the darkened windows of the restaurant from across the street, *The Slammin' Sushi*. Most Japanese inspired restaurants used blacked out windows to aid in the ambience of the inside décor. It was also the perfect hiding spot for the set of eyes that watched the three friends entering the café, trying to find the truth. A truth that would find them all on its own.

* * *

After second breakfast, the three friends went their separate ways to prepare for tonight. Kevin made the phone call to Nancy asking for her help. She was quick with ideas on what her and Adam would be able to do. Breaking the law wasn't a huge concern with Nancy as it was with Kevin, something he thought they should talk about once everything cooled down.

He wasn't as experienced in the ways of having a relationship. In fact, his last serious girlfriend was Nancy back in high school. They both liked the same movies and TV shows. She was the person who first suggested to Kevin that there should be a convention just for action movies. When Kevin embarked on creating *Act-Con*, he thought about contacting Nancy to help out, but they're breakup was not pleasant, and he figured she'd be more likely to hurt him rather than help.

Only after Kevin's first and last *Act-Con* was disrupted by the Scout's attempted bombing, did he consider reconnecting with Nancy even if it was just as friends. After high school, Nancy joined the army and served several tours overseas before leaving and entering the private sector. Adept at computers and a penchant for gadgets, she had no trouble finding work at any number of corporations as part of their security force. She doesn't talk about that work much with Kevin.

Kevin liked Nancy, but she scared him. He never remembered why they broke up senior year. They were fighting a lot towards the end, so the reason was probably more than one. Regardless, they ended it before graduation and hadn't spoken since Adam asked her for help with the Scout business four months ago.

Now he was bringing her into the agency. Combining his two worlds, which wasn't always a good thing, and this was yet another worry on Kevin's mind as he walked towards his parent's front door and waved goodbye to Becky from across the street.

Becky tapped an imaginary watch on her wrist to remind Kevin about their assigned time to meet back up tonight. The plan was to head to the hospital late in the night in hopes of gaining access to Jane Doe without an issue. Kevin turned his wave into a 'thumbs up' but realized he may be revealing their mission to the two uniformed officers sitting in a police cruiser in front of Adam's house. The officers were already parked at the house when they returned from their lunch. Kenney had the force working in shifts to protect Adam. Given Adam's reputation amongst the men in blue, Kevin figured no one was happy about the babysitting job.

Kevin's fears of revealing their plan was unfounded, as the officers were not paying attention to anything happening outside the cruiser. They each had their phones out and their heads were down, no doubt checking their *Facebook* feeds. Kevin retreated into his house.

Adam stood at his front window. He watched Kevin walk into his house. He studied the officers in the cruiser. He made note that the yard needed to be mowed, something he promised his mother he'd do when she let him live there. In fact, he had to promise to keep the house and yard in 'good shape' when he phoned her about staying at the home he grew up. This was the first and only home he knew when they moved to Hilldale and the one he left when he ventured out of the small New England town to find his calling. After not finding anything remotely resembling something he loved, he returned a broken man to his childhood home to find his mom had moved to Florida to escape the cold, dreary Northeast winters.

After Becky closed the front door behind her, he returned his attention to the cops parked outside the house. He watched them for thirty minutes without break. He studied their movements. He knew when they would check their phones before they even reached into their pockets for them.

It was mid-afternoon. Adam had time before making his trek to Brookville. The back door opened, as he had anticipated since he left it unlocked and instructed Nancy to come through the house that way.

"Where'd you park?" Adam asked, not turning around.

"You already know where. You told me to park there," Nancy replied. She didn't like answering questions that the person asking already knew the answer. It was a waste of time. She joined Adam in watching the cops.

"They could see you," Adam said.

"Doubtful. And who cares? They have no legal grounds to enter your home. Not without your permission or a warrant."

Adam nodded. "I agree, but they could wonder why I have a visitor."

"They'd probably think it was Becky. Here to make out with you."

Adam coughed. He was caught off-guard. "What? We're not..."

Nancy laughed. "I know. Relax. But I wouldn't be surprised if a few people in this town didn't think that. Including Becky's husband."

"Jesus. And Kevin likes you?"

She punched Adam in the arm. Hard. He winced.

He rubbed his arm, to wipe away the pain. "So. What's our plan?"

"Sneak out the back. Go across the backyard to the neighbors..."

"I meant for the police station," he turned to face Nancy. "I know how we're leaving here."

"Obviously." She pulled a rolled-up sheet of paper from her backpack, something Adam just realized she was sporting.

Nancy moved to the coffee table in the living room. She swept aside various knick-knacks left over from Adam's mother's decorative tastes. Adam didn't bother to move anything or dust or any large amount of cleaning. This was evident when the dust induced a sneezing fit in Nancy.

He realized he wasn't living up to the bargain he struck with his mother about making sure the house was in good shape. First the lawn needed tending to and now the living room. He shuddered when he thought of the bathrooms.

"Bless you," Adam said after Nancy's sneezing fit ended.

"I'd rather you just clean the house once in a while. Jesus." She complained.

She flattened out the large sheet of paper to reveal schematics of the Brookville Sheriff's Station. A one level building with a basement that's used only for storage. The quaintness of the sheriff station matched the smallness of the town of Brookville.

"Did you hack into a database for this?" Adam asked.

"Do you want me to answer that?"

Adam thought about it. "Maybe after this is all done."

"Nervous?" Nancy asked.

"About breaking in? I guess. I just need to find out what happened to Fred."

"I remember Fred Thompson. Kind of an asshole in high school," Nancy said. Adam paused. He didn't know how to respond. He always had fond memories of Thompson. She continued. "No, I meant are you nervous about someone wanting to kill you?"

"Concerned, I guess. That's probably more accurate."

"You get used to it."

"Really?"

Nancy nodded. She studied the schematic as she spoke, "In war, everyone wants to kill you. I served in a country for two years with a bullseye on my back. After a while, you just accept it."

Adam never considered Nancy's insight. He never considered anything about Nancy except that Kevin liked her and she had cool gadgets they could use to spy on cheating husbands. "What about after? When you got home."

She stood up. Stared Adam in the eye. "That's worst. You have to change your default settings."

He nodded. "You really like him, don't you?"

"Kevin reminds me of what I used to be. Back in school. I need to find that person or at least part of her."

"And when you find her? What happens then?" Adam asked.

Nancy smiled. "How about we figure out how to get into that sheriff station first?" She deflected with ease.

Adam took the hint. He turned his attention to the schematic.

# Chapter 8
## Hospital Visit

Becky spent the day toiling around the house by completing random chores in an effort to keep herself busy. She scrubbed the oven clean in order to not think about the inevitable confrontation she would have with Mark. The attic was dusted in an effort to ignore everything wrong with the impending attempt to talk with the highly protected Jane Doe at Hilldale Hospital. Even the mini-van was cleaned out to calm Becky's nerves as she worried about Adam's fate if they failed.

Every so often, she'd glance at the police car parked in front of Adam's house. Even though the protection wasn't for her, she still felt a bit safer than usual having a police presence on her street. Ever since the events with the Scout, including her daughter being kidnapped, Becky existed in a state of consistent concern. Concern for her family, for Adam and Kevin and, right now, for her marriage.

She didn't want to choose between the agency and her family. It wasn't that the choice was a hard one to make. On the contrary, the choice was easy. She loved playing detective, as Mark would call it and it was true. Even though they were calling themselves the Parker Detective Agency, there was really no financial stability or legitimacy to any of their work. It was, in fact, the three of them playing detective.

With the exception of stopping the Scout, their work had been uneventful up until Adam solved the Professor Caulfield murder. The fight in the chemistry lab was scary and exciting. Most people would run and hide ion the face of that kind of danger, but Becky was of a different ilk. She never panicked. Her only concern the other night was trying to find a better angle of attack, which she found when she entered the room from the door behind the crazed student. She touched her eye as she thought of that night. Still sore. The bruise had faded from its purplish hue to an ugly yellow.

Becky reveled in her role with the agency. Kevin often called her the muscle and even though she'd outwardly argue that term, she secretly loved it. She was the muscle. She rubbed her yellow-stained eye a bit more. It was painful the harder she pushed, but it didn't bother her. She smiled. All her consternation. All her despair over having to choose between her family and the agency. All of it was because of how much she loved being part of it. The aches and pains. The chase. The revelations. It was exciting. It was what she always wanted to do. She hated having to give it up.

That's the reason she hemmed and hawed about leaving. She already knew she would choose her family over the detective life. Making the choice wasn't her problem, it was *having* to make the choice. It was the biggest reason why she fought Mark so hard when it came to his concerns about the agency. She argued with Mark in order to prevent the inevitable. She fought off his concern at every turn, but it wore her down. She understood his anger. This wasn't the woman he married. When he used that reasoning in an argument, even though she empathized with Mark, Becky would go on the offensive about how people change all the time and how marriage is about making that change work for each other. In short, her argument was that Mark would have to get over it.

Once the afternoon turned into early evening, Becky rallied herself back up for a fight with Mark. He strolled in through the front door and dropped his messenger bag on the chair in the living room.

"How was work?" Becky asked.

"Uneventful," Mark offered, but nothing more. He made his way to the kitchen to grab a beer from the refrigerator.

The kids were in their rooms doing homework, at least Becky pretended they were studying, but the truth lied somewhere between texting and video games. She followed Mark into the kitchen.

"I have to go out tonight," she said.

"Yeah, I figured." Mark twisted the bottle-cap from the beer. He flicked it into the sink. He took a long swig from the bottle.

"No fight?" Becky asked.

He shrugged. "Would it matter?"

Mark returned to the living room. He sat on the couch and opened the messenger bag. Case files from work. He had a trial next week, so prep was his main focus these days.

She watched him get his papers in order. He drank from his beer. He opened the laptop and tapped away at the keyboard. He never looked up from the screen. Becky waited for him to look up. Some kind of acknowledgement of her presence. But it never came.

"I'm starting dinner." Becky skulked to the kitchen.

Mark grunted his assent.

\* \* \*

Dinner was quiet. Idle chat about school and upcoming events – bake sales, dances, PTO meetings. Becky hadn't been to a PTO meeting since last school year. They didn't seem important to her anymore. Dinner ended, and everyone returned to their weekday routine. The routine was what got everyone through the week. Get up. Go to work or school. Come home. Homework. Work. Watch TV. Off to bed. Every night. The same thing. Becky despised the routine.

She grabbed her jacket, a light wind-breaker. Fall was here, but summer was hanging on like it always did in the

Northeast. Kevin insisted on driving tonight and Becky appreciated the break, so she was to meet him at his house. She turned to say goodbye to Mark, but he was entrenched in his work partly to avoid this exact moment. At least, that's what Becky figured. She gave up trying to connect with Mark. She closed the door behind her and headed for Kevin's home.

As she crossed the street, she glanced at the police cruiser parked in front of Adam's house. Two silhouettes sat in the front seat. They were still, but Becky felt their eyes on her. She waved. They didn't wave back. Dealing with rude cops wasn't new for Becky, especially since teaming up with Adam. Most of the police didn't like them butting their noses in on cases. Becky knew they weren't thrilled about babysitting Adam, but she didn't understand why their rudeness extended to her.

She made it to Kevin's front steps when the door opened as quick as it was slammed shut. Kevin bounced out of the house. He changed his red t-shirt in favor of a green t-shirt that had a character from the popular *Minecraft* game. Becky knew of *Minecraft* from watching her son, Jake, play the game on his tablet, but she didn't know any of the characters. The tablet was a birthday gift from her mother that was not well received by Becky, seeing that Jake spent most of his days on it.

It made sense that Kevin played the game, too. All Kevin did was play video games, work and solve crimes. It was the life he always wanted.

"I don't always play video games." Kevin said, reading Becky's thoughts.

She was stunned. "Did you... No, right? I wasn't saying..."

He cut her off. "You were gawking at my shirt for a good 20 seconds. I knew what you were thinking."

"I could've been thinking about how that dude on your shirt reminded me to open up the game and - build stuff?"

"You had your default pity face. You would've been found out eventually."

Becky's kids made fun of her for the same reason. She wasn't able to hide her feelings. She lied and lied often, but her facial expressions always revealed her true feelings. Eventually, Jake and Caitlyn surmised that their mother had a default pity face that first appeared when she disapproved of something but didn't know how to lie or be nice about it. Becky didn't believe them until they provided examples and soon, she had no option but to concede. Word spread to Kevin and Adam, of course, and they teased her about it just as much as her kids. Adam more so than Kevin.

"I'm going to ignore that, so as not to bruise my hand on your face," she threatened.

"So violent." Kevin smiled. He looked at the police car. "They still in there?"

Becky turned around to have another look. "Haven't moved most of the day. I waved, but they ignored me."

"Probably a Kenney directive." Kevin waved, but the cops didn't budge. "Screw 'em. Let's find this Jane Doe." He unlocked the car doors with the key fob.

Becky opened the passenger side door. "And how are we going to do that, exactly?"

"I don't know. I'm making this up as…"

"Stop." Becky held up her hand. "What did I tell you about movie quotes?"

Kevin's shoulders sagged. "Not to do them," he said, repeating the command Becky laid out over and over again.

"Good." She hopped in the car.

"I'm just happy you knew it was a movie quote." Kevin shut the door behind him as he turned the key in the ignition.

\* \* \*

The hospital, on the other side of town, was technically still in Hilldale but bordered the neighboring town of Wellsboro. Wellsboro was known as the town where the shore and inland borders met. It wasn't rare to find a storm pass through the state and Hilldale would be drenched with rain, while Wellsboro residents shoveled out three inches for their morning commute.

The hospital served much of the Southern Connecticut area towns and cities. Compared to the other hospitals in the state, it was definitely smaller in stature and staff. The rumor in the state capital was that Hilldale Hospital may close up in the coming years since *Yale-New Haven* had seen exponential growth over the past decade and much of the area residents sought care at their facility.

The drive through the center of town was an easy one. They passed Kevin's family's hardware store. He looked, out of instinct, making sure the lights were turned off. He developed the same trait as his father. Check for the lights. Always check to see if the lights are on. He cursed under his breath. He was becoming his father.

They still didn't have a plan for how to gain access to Jane Doe. Each took turns offering suggestions, but the plans always ended in silence once the question of how to get around the cops guarding the door reared its head.

The car pulled into a visitor spot in front of the hospital. At the entrance, several police cars were parked. Wellsboro and Hilldale.

"I don't like this," Becky muttered.

"We have to do it. We need to find out what she knows." Kevin scanned the entrance. "She'd be in ICU, right?"

"Maybe. I don't know."

"Well, we need to find that out." Kevin said.

"How exactly?"

Another police car from Wellsboro pulled up and two officers exited. They adjusted their gun belts and uniform as they entered the front entrance. Kevin turned to Becky. "They look like next shift."

"Next shift for what?" Becky asked. She stopped, realizing what Kevin was saying. "Wait. They *do* look like next shift."

She was out of the car fast. Slamming the door in her wake. She quickly covered the distance to the front entrance. Kevin stumbled behind her. He was not as fast out of the car, as he tried to catch up. He already knew Becky's plan. Follow the two Wellsboro officers to Jane Doe. Simple enough. Kevin's shortness of breath was not so simple. He stopped to catch his breath as Becky casually walked through the revolving front doors, about twenty feet behind the officers.

Kevin forced himself to move. He stepped through the front entrance and found a quiet lobby. It was night, so visiting hours were coming to an end and with less staff on duty, it made for a muted atmosphere.

He found Becky standing in front of the elevators. Her eyes were trained on the digital read-out above the doors, counting the floors.

"We may catch a break with Wellsboro P.D. here," she said.

"If we can find them. Why?" Kevin asked.

"They don't know us. I'd imagine Kenney has his people on the lookout for us. He has trust issues when it comes to Adam."

"Can't blame him there. We're doing exactly what he said not to do."

The digital read-out stopped on '5'. Becky pointed at it. "Got 'em."

She slapped the arrow button point up and they waited for another elevator to come for them.

Kevin looked to the plastic-coated sign on the wall. He pointed at it. Then he nudged Becky. "*ICU*. Fifth floor."

"You want a medal?" Becky asked.

"Damn. That's not cool," he replied. "But if you're offering."

"Sorry. It's been a rough couple of days." She rubbed her forehead, relieving the tension swirling in her head.

"Are you and Mark going to be okay?" Kevin asked.

She sighed. "I think so. It's just…" She looked to Kevin and knew he wasn't ready for her decision that this was her last case.

The elevator beeped. Doors opened. They exited into the hallway. The conversation was over. The doors opened to the fifth floor. The automatic doors of the ICU were directly in front of them, but they were locked from the inside. A call button was on the wall next to the door. If they hit that, they'd need a good reason to enter, so they waited.

Kevin looked through the small slit in the door that was technically called a window, but Kevin knew otherwise. He made out the nurses at the main desk and several empty gurneys in the hallways, but no police.

"Where'd those cops go?" Kevin asked.

"Maybe she's in the back of the unit?" Becky offered with zero confidence in her assessment. "We sure she's in the ICU?"

Kevin paused. He looked up at a sign dangling from the ceiling. A big arrow pointed towards the automatic doors and read: *ICU*. Another arrow pointed left and read: *Radiology*. The right arrow read: *Behavioral*.

"She was found in the basement. Dirty, like she'd been there for a while. Giggling, right?" Kevin said.

"Yeah. They thought she was on something."

"What if she wasn't on something and that was the problem," Kevin said.

"What do you mean?"

"What if she needed medication? You wouldn't go to *ICU* if you have mental issues."

"Mental issues?" Becky asked.

"What? Is that, not right?"

"It's a bit insensitive."

"Mental problems?"

"Wrong word to change, buddy."

"Shit."

"Let's go. I'll help you figure out how to be a good person along the way."

The arrow was misleading as they walked the length of the hospital to the other side of the building to find *Behavioral* and another automatic door. Kevin looked through the small window on the door and this time they found the right section. He counted four police officers in the hallway and another two sitting in front of a room. The door was shut. He relayed all this to Becky.

"Are they all Hilldale police?" Becky asked.

"I can't tell."

"Look at the patches on the sleeve."

"Patches? Why?" Kevin asked.

"Because each police department has a different logo."

"But I don't know which logo is for what town."

Becky smiled. "I do."

Kevin turned from the door. "How do you know that?"

She shrugged. "Random assimilation of information. I get bored at home when they kids are at school and all the chores are done. I surf the web."

"And different police insignias are what you surf the internet about?"

"Will you just tell me what the patches look like?" Becky held her hand up, guiding Kevin back to the door.

He returned to the small window. "The four in the hallway have the same patch. Looks like a Christmas tree without the lights on it."

"That's Wellsboro." Becky said. "That's an evergreen tree, by the way. Apparently, Wellsboro is lousy with them."

"The two at the door..." Kevin squinted. "I can't tell what it is. But they're different from the Wellsboro cops."

"Makes sense. Kenney probably has Hilldale's finest guarding the girl and Wellsboro for support." Becky leaned against the wall. Kevin leaned on the opposite wall. The double doors between them.

Kevin asked, "Now what?"

Becky had no answers. They waited. Again.

# Chapter 9
## Visit to Brookville

Adam and Nancy argued about their plan of attack on the Brookville Sheriff Station throughout the afternoon before realizing that nightfall had arrived and with it, the time for them to leave the house. The police cruiser was still parked in front of Adam's house. Adam pulled down a few slats of the blinds that were drawn over his front window. He studied the dark silhouettes of the officers. They had their heads down. Neither moved. He figured they were looking at their phones again.

"Hilldale Police Department at its best," Nancy said as she looked through the other window.

"They're okay," Adam defended them. "You don't like them?"

Nancy shrugged. "They're always hassling me."

"Could it be the small arsenal you keep in your basement?"

"I have permits for all of that stuff. I'm a collector."

"And a hacker. And an anarchist. And I'm pretty sure you're growing weed in that basement of yours as well."

Nancy blinked. "Well, shit, Parker. You've got all the answers, don't you?"

"Just observant. I'm curious. What does Kevin think about it?"

"We don't talk about it much, if you know what I mean." She winked.

Adam grimaced. "C'mon. I don't need to hear that."

"Then don't ask about my business."

"If your business gets my best friend in trouble with the law, I'm going to have a problem with it."

"Says the guy who's consistently in trouble with the police for obstruction and who's about to commit a felony crime by breaking into a sheriff's station."

"While I see your point, I am trying to stop my own murder."

Nancy took a breath. She was done with the conversation. "Can we get going?"

Adam held out his hand guiding Nancy to the back door. "Shall we?"

She slung her backpack over her shoulder and headed for the back door, careful not to make too much noise. Adam took one more glance at the cruiser through the front window. Still no movement. For some reason, it bothered him, but he stored that feeling for now. They had a mission.

The path to Nancy's car was straight, but not exactly clear. They would have to get over the hedges that separated Adam's backyard from his neighbor's yard. There was a crab apple tree that was close enough for them to climb, thus giving them a launch point to get over the hedges. The entire yard at the foot of the tree was covered in fallen apples. Most of them rotted out and picked at by squirrels.

After fumbling on a few of those apples, Nancy turned to Adam, "Jesus, Parker. Clean the yard much?"

"All the time. You don't like?" Adam smiled.

Nancy rolled her eyes. She grabbed the lowest branch on the tree and climbed. She was quick in her ascent. Ending it with a jump, then a tuck and roll into the neighbor's yard. Her army training kicked in. Adam wasn't quite as adept in his turn. He struggled to climb the tree, slipping a few times. As he jumped from a perch above the hedge, he lost his footing. He half-fell, half-jumped from the tree, scraping his back on the hedges on the way down and landing on the neighbor's yard with a thud. He cried out in pain.

Nancy stood over him. "That looked like it hurt."

"Shut-up." Adam struggled to get himself up. He rubbed his back as he walked ahead of her.

Nancy stifled a smile as she followed him towards her car. They were on the highway in no time, heading for Brookville. Neither speaking until a few exits into the drive.

"So, who do you think wants to kill you?" Nancy asked.

Adam shrugged. "I have no idea. I just got back in town four months ago. I didn't have time to make any enemies."

"You made plenty back in the day."

"What's that mean?"

"Don't get me wrong, Parker. I like you all right. But back in school, you were another kind of prick."

"What? I was okay. I was just popular."

"No shit. And you made sure to let everyone know that."

"Pulling a few pranks is what teenagers do."

"Not exactly what you did, but yeah. Teenagers do stupid things. I get it. But you could get mean with the best of them."

Adam was silent. He wanted to argue but thought better of it. He remembered the things he did in high school. He knew the type of person he had become back then. Looking back, he wasn't proud of it, but his path in high school wasn't much different than every other teenager growing up back then. Everyone regretted something from their youth. But those regrets don't equate to death threats when you grow up, right?

"I don't know who wants to kill me," Adam said.

"Maybe not, but you have a good idea, don't you? That's why we're driving to Brookville. That's why you're letting Becky and Kevin chase the Jane Doe lead. You don't think that's going anywhere. You think Brookville holds the key to your suspicion."

He smirked. "Maybe *you* should be the detective."

"Do you think we could meet up with some trouble?" Nancy asked, almost wishing for a positive answer to her question.

"At the sheriff's station? Probably not. I mean, I hope not. And I don't think the Jane Doe lead is fruitless. No leads are truly a dead-end until we check them out. Someone killed my friend, Nancy. And if it was to get to me, well that's something I need to discover soon. Before they get to another friend."

"Kevin?" Nancy said. Her tone held a tinge of nervousness behind it, even though she tried to hide it from Adam.

He felt it. "In this line of work, we're all targets."

"I should be with him then. I should be protecting him."

"He can take care of...", Nancy whipped her head around. She glared away Adam's reply. He nodded. "You're right. He's not good with that sort of stuff, but Becky is with him and she *is* good at it."

Nancy calmed down. "Okay. You're right. She's tough."

"She can kick my ass."

She scoffed. "So, can I. Big deal."

Adam paused. Stunned, but then he smiled. That turned into a laugh. Nancy joined him. Adam couldn't stop laughing. He knew she was right.

* * *

They parked in an empty lot that was attached to a rundown strip mall containing more vacant storefronts than active businesses. The sheriff station was located on a small plot of land directly across from the strip mall, which made the parking lot the perfect spot to spend a long night to watch the comings and goings of the Brookville Sheriff's Department. As soon as they parked the car, Nancy made a dash for the convenience store located at the far end of the strip mall. They needed nourishment to keep them awake.

Several hours later, Adam finished off his third mini-can of *Pringles* when he caught sight of someone familiar. Sheriff Copeland exited the building. "Finally. I thought he was going to close up the place."

"Who?" Nancy shot up from her seat. She had been laying back trying to get a few moments of sleep.

"The old guy. Beard. He's limping across the lawn to his car in the lot." Adam pointed out the thick frame of Sheriff Copeland. He hadn't noticed the limp the last time he spoke with Copeland at the cemetery.

"He doesn't look so mean. Kevin said he was mean."

"Well, he wasn't exactly rolling out the welcome mat when we first met him," Adam said and then changed course. "And Kevin shouldn't be talking about a case with you."

"But now I'm part of it, so who cares?"

"But you weren't part of it before. He's revealing secrets. I can't have that. Who knows what else you might know."

Nancy chuckled. "Oh, I know a lot."

Adam did a double-take. This whole trip was turning into one revelation after another. He refocused his attention back on Sheriff Copeland, who was already inside his car and pulling out of the stationhouse's parking lot. He shot out his hand and waved goodbye to a few straggling deputies by the front door.

"So, the boss is away." Nancy reached for her backpack from the back seat. "It's time we get to play."

"Around back?" Adam asked.

"If those plans were right, the back door is a straight shot to the Sheriff's office. Seems like the easiest spot for us to access their computer system."

"Dammit.," Adam cursed to himself. "Why didn't we just hack in remotely?"

"The encryption is probably extremely difficult, given the influence John Thornton has over this town," Nancy replied.

Adam paused. "You already tried."

"Of course, I did," She nodded. "You think I wanted to take this ride with you?"

"Thanks," he changed subjects. "How much do you know about John Thornton?" Adam opened his door.

Becky followed suit. Careful to not slam it shut to avoid raising suspicion from across the street. "Same thing anyone knows. Gazillionaire who owns most of this town. No one knows what he does, which fascinates conspiracy theorists like me."

"Aren't most rich people private, eccentric and fascinating?"

"Thornton is all that and more," Nancy said. The excitement in her voice was noticeable.

They crossed the street. Traffic was nonexistent. Residents were not enjoying the night life in Brookville tonight. Even the crickets were quiet. Adam looked down the road to make sure a fog wasn't rolling in to portend their doom. "I've always avoided coming here, if I could. Even when I was a kid. Even now, I feel like we're being watched."

"We probably are. One of the things I read is that the entire town is under surveillance. Something to do with an experiment from decades ago, long since stopped. But the cameras remained. Still recording."

Adam paused. "Maybe the experiment never really ended. They just let people think that."

Nancy smiled. "Now, you sound like me."

Adam didn't like that. "The sooner we get out of there, the better."

"I've heard stories. None of it makes sense, but it always ends the same. Cover up."

"And this is based on?" Adam asked.

"I said... Stories. The dark net is filled with them. Brookville is mentioned in several journals across the globe about its weird history. And Thornton is at the center of it. You never heard any of this?"

Adam shook his head. "I mean. Growing up, you hear all sorts of things, but you don't believe it. Strange sounds in the night. Kids going missing in a corn maze."

"That was when we were in school. I remember that."

"But how do you know that's real?"

"How do you know it's not?" She shot back.

"We could look it up. Google. Yahoo." Adam said.

"I have. Everything is mired in a designed fiction. I could fill podcasts on techniques that are used to confuse anyone searching for the truth."

He stopped on the sidewalk. They were in front of the sheriff station. The deputies who were outside before had returned to their desks. Adam held up his hands. "You're a little intense, right now."

"It's kind of a passion."

"It's great. It really is, but one problem at a time. Let's find out what happened to my friend and then we'll tackle whatever X-Files shit is happening in this town."

He walked to the side of the stationhouse. He looked for the side door. Nancy followed suit, careful not to hurry and call attention to themselves. Once they reached the edge of the stationhouse, they casually strolled along the perimeter. It wasn't any bigger than Hilldale's smallest downtown building, but it was still formidable.

Adam scanned the windows for movement, waiting for a deputy to look outside and spy two dark-clothed people walking slowly around the building. But that never happened. No one looked outside. No one exited the building. Even foot traffic on the sidewalk had dissipated.

Nancy grabbed his arm and led him behind the stationhouse. Beyond the parking lot, there was a small dimly lit back door. The stairs leading up to the door were covered in cigarette butts and spilled beer. It smelled like the back patio of a frat house. Nancy examined the door handle.

Adam kept lookout. The parking lot had three cars. The night crew settling in for a quiet night. He took note of the slanted basketball net sitting on the other side of the lot. Rusted from the elements.

Nancy pulled a small leather case from her backpack. Her lock pick set. She went to work on the key hole of the door handle. Adam noticed her tongue curling up from her mouth to her upper lip. Concentration caused many tells. Before he could make a comment: *Click!*

She slowly pulled the door open and the noise from inside the office filtered out to the back steps. Adam leaned in to take the first look. The hallway was clear and brightly lit. He didn't anticipate the great lighting and thus, more chance of them being seen, but there was no turning back now. He leaned away from the door, closer to Nancy.

He whispered, "Copeland's office should be five doors down on the right."

"After you," Nancy said as she placed the lock pit set in her backpack.

Adam took a moment, then a deep breath. He entered the stationhouse. The reality of their felonious act suddenly hit him. He cursed under his breath. A large sense of dread overtook him. He heard Nancy giggling behind him. She clearly wasn't hiding her concern. Adam ignored the giggles and his own worries and pushed through. They crept, slightly crouched and somewhat upright, down the hallway. Only muffled voices and the ringing of the phone was heard off to the left from the main room.

Their toughest challenge. The entrance to the main room was on their left. It was a clear look into the hallway from the main room. In order for Adam and Nancy to get to

Copeland's office, they'd have to make sure no one was looking in their direction as they dashed across the opening. It was a big risk.

He turned back to Nancy, "We should've created distraction out front."

"Relax," She shook her head. "If we did that, this place would be lousy with cops. Even worse, if they figured out it was bogus. They'd search the place and find us with our hands in the cookie jar. Keeping it as quiet as possible is what we want."

"I don't like it."

"It's too late."

*Flush!* A door along the right side of the hallway opened and a deputy entered the hallway a few feet ahead of the two amateur burglars. He was heavyset and dark-skinned. He tucked a newspaper back under his arm as he adjusted his pants. His back was to Adam and Nancy the whole time.

They froze in their spots, as if stuck in glue. The deputy cleared his throat and adjusted his shirt, finishing the tuck job he started. He remained turned away from them. He paused and slowly turned around to see Adam staring right at him.

"What the…"

Nancy stepped forward. A small device in her hand. She shoved it in front of the deputy's face and it chirped and flashed. The deputy's eyes closed and toppled forward towards Adam. Instinctively, he moved to the side. The deputy crashed to the ground.

"You killed him," Adam whispered as loud as he could without detection. He quickly glanced through the doorway to the main room. No movement. No screams for help. No one heard the deputy hit the floor.

"Relax. This is an alpha-wave generator. It causes a person to go to sleep."

"Where'd you get that?"

"I have a friend in DARPA, but you didn't hear that from me."

"Wait. Isn't that from a movie?" Adam asked.

"Where do you think the army got the idea?" She grabbed the deputy's legs. "We really should move him now."

Adam wrapped his arms underneath the large man's shoulders. They struggled to one of the many doors they had passed. A janitor's closet. When the opened the door, Adam sized up the space. He looked to the deputy in their hands and the closet several times before declaring, "He's not going to fit."

"We'll make him fit," Nancy assured him.

Making him fit required Adam to hold the deputy up on his feet and walking him into the closet. Adam leaned him face first against a shelf of toilet paper and paper towels. He shoved his hand onto the deputy's back and stepped away. He took a wide stance to brace the weight of the deputy to keep him in a standing position as Adam prepared to hop into the hallway. Adam bent his knees to prepare for his escape and to be quick enough for Nancy to shut the door before the deputy fell backwards into the hallway. Nancy leaned forward. She held the handle of the closet door. They stared at each other. Counting down in their heads with nods. Adam bolted into the hall, as Nancy pushed the door shut as the deputy fell back.

Boom!

The door shook from the weight of the falling deputy. Adam cringed. "He's going to have a headache."

"And memory loss." She smiled. "He might even wet himself."

"Are you supposed to have that thing?" Adam pointed to the alpha wave generator in Nancy's back pocket.

"I'm not supposed to have a lot of things. Better you don't worry about it." She patted him on the shoulder and made her way to Copeland's office, not bothering to pause before crossing the opening that led to the main room. Adam reached out to stop her, but Nancy was gone.

He ducked against the wall. He closed his eyes, cringing from the expectation of what was to come. He waited for the shouts. He waited for the calls to "Stop!" Or "Freeze!" Or anything! But nothing happened. He opened his eyes to find Nancy looking back at him, on the other side of the opened doorway. She tapped her wrist, as if a watch was there, demanding Adam to hurry up and knock it off.

He sighed. He gave a look through the opened doorway. The voices were no longer coming from the room. They moved. The coast was clear. Adam straightened up. Regained a shred of his confidence and crossed to meet Nancy.

"Gee. You made it. Thank God." The sarcasm was strong with Nancy.

Adam ignored her. He made straight for Copeland's door. He checked the handle. Unlocked. He walked right into the office and waited for Nancy to join him.

Once inside, they kept the lights off. The lights from the hallway was enough and if they kept relatively low, searching through the files would be uninterrupted. Nancy took a seat at the desk. She tapped away at the computer.

A screen popped up asking for a username and password.

"Jesus." Nancy muttered.

"What?"

"I was right. This system is super advanced for a small-town sheriff's department."

"Can you get in?"

Nancy scoffed. "Watch this."

She pulled a USB drive from her pocket and plugged it into one of the many USB ports on the computer tower. Immediately a window on the desktop opened and a program started. The entire screen flashed to black and returned to the same login screen. The window with the program remained open, but the program had paused. There was a username and password in the window. Nancy copied the information from the window and pasted it into the proper slots on the login screen. She clicked *enter.*

"We're in."

"You scare me," Adam said.

"You're lucky I'm with Kevin."

He didn't argue. Instead, he pointed to the searchable file database program on the desktop. Nancy was way ahead of him. She searched the files for Fred Thompson and immediately a folder popped up. She clicked through and opened up a folder named *Pics.*

Instantly the screen was flooded with thumbnails of the crime scene. Adam's face contorted from the images of the macabre scene, but soon his observational mind took over. He pointed to one photo. "Can you blow this up?"

Nancy clicked on it. The image grew to reveal the back of Fred and the tree he was leaning on. "What are you looking for?"

"I don't know," Adam replied. "Can you cycle through them?"

"I have a better idea. Why don't I just copy the folder to a flash." She pulled another USB drive from her pocket and found another open port on the tower.

Adam nodded. "Good idea. The less time here, the better."

"You think?"

Adam walked around the office. He studied the books on the shelves and the pictures on the wall. A few diplomas from Copeland's past. The pictures were a mix of personal and professional, the latter usual marking a milestone in Copeland's career. He found a photo of what looked like Copeland's family. Smiling wife, smiling children sans one. A teenager with that disaffected teenage glare. Adam knew it well.

"Done." Nancy gathered her gear. She slung the backpack over her shoulder and headed for the door.

Adam followed her lead. "You got everything?"

"And then some." She winked.

Adam didn't want to decipher what that meant as they stepped softly back down the hallway. Careful around the doorway to the main room again, but still no sign of the night crew at the Brookville Sheriff Station. Adam thought they might've got called out. Maybe one of those mysteries that people from other towns wonder so much about. Secret experiment gone wrong? Someone's pet dragon let loose? Donuts are eating people?

Adam didn't care. He had his own murder to stop.

# Chapter 10
## Jane Doe

Across the way from the double door entrance to the *Behavioral* section of the hospital was a collection of chairs. Technically, it was considered a waiting area, but in reality, it was just a place to sit. Kevin was asleep in one of the chairs. This time of night, not many visitors were using the area, so Becky and Kevin set up shop waiting for a plan to reveal itself to them. The six officers remained in the hallway beyond the automatic double doors. Every time the doors opened up, Becky caught a glimpse of the cops from both towns talking, some would look her way, but didn't really expect the two barely awake people in the waiting room to be a threat.

Kevin snorted himself awake, nearly falling off the chair. He looked around and found Becky staring at him. "You saw that?"

She ignored him. "What're we going to do? We have to talk to her?"

"The cops are still there?" Kevin asked.

"Haven't moved in over two hours. And neither have we," Becky stood up and faced Kevin. "We need to do something."

He held up his arms. "I've got nothing. Adam is the one that comes up with the plans."

"But they fail most of the time."

"Yes. But he still comes up with them."

She clenched her hands in frustration. "Then what would Adam do?"

Kevin shrugged. It was his turn to stand up. He placed his hands on his lower back and pushed, stretching whatever muscles lay dormant. He rolled his neck back and forth. He had developed a kink in his neck from awkwardly falling asleep on the chair.

He eventually walked the hallway while thinking aloud. "He might look to cause a distraction. Get the cops to leave the hallway. Maybe pull a fire alarm. Cause a fire. Start a fight. Push me into someone else which would then cause a fight."

The double door opened. An orderly pushed an older man, upper body propped up, on a gurney through. The man politely smiled as he spotted Kevin. A few doctors and nurses crossed the hall, causing the orderly to bring the gurney to a stop. The traffic passed in front.

"Really?" Becky asked. She eyed the gurney.

"It's happened." Kevin said. He turned around, back to the gurney, "Works most of the time."

Without thinking, Becky shoved him. Hard. Kevin fell back and slammed into the gurney. The gurney, the patient and Kevin all toppled over and smacked the ground. The patient's smile disappeared. He screamed in pain. Immediately, the orderly worked to replace the gurney to its upright position and help the older man back on.

"What's your problem?" He yelled at Kevin, not really looking for an answer.

Kevin struggled to pull himself up. His back sore from slamming into the metal frame of the rolling bed. The doctors and nurses who passed before, returned to help. A few helped Kevin regain his footing and then proceeded to yell at him, echoing the orderly's anger.

Kevin shouted back. He tried to explain that it wasn't his fault, but by that time, Becky moved closer to the double doors that led to the *Behavioral* unit. She made eye contact with Kevin, who knew what to do.

He smiled at Becky. Then got louder. He shoved the first person in his face, which happened to be a doctor. He hit the ground. Kevin stood over him. Shouting obscenities. Calls for security rang out from the nurses.

On cue, the double doors opened up and both Wellsboro and Hilldale officers piled out to address the screaming and shouting in the hallway. Becky slid through the opening just as the double doors closed. She was alone in the hallway. The muted sounds of people shouting came from behind the automatic doors.

Becky remained close to the wall until she came upon the now unguarded door to Jane Doe. She slowly pushed open the door and entered the room. She found the girl from *Lonnie's* basement, Jane Doe, resting in her bed. Her black, stringy hair lay still. Her chest slowly moving up and down. She was sleeping. An IV was inserted in her arm, as she received a medicine drip of some kind. The sounds of an older television show came from the wall mounted TV. A game show that Becky couldn't place but had seen before.

Becky approached the bed. The girl's eyes were closed, but once Becky was by her side, the eyes slowly opened. She turned to face Becky.

Each stared at the other. Becky not sure what to say. "What's your name?"

The girl turned away. Focused on the TV.

Becky figured that was a stupid question and one that had already been asked countless times by doctors, nurses and police. She tried a new tactic.

"Adam Parker."

The girl turned her head again. She faced Becky with the smile.

"Parker. Parker. Parker." She repeated over and over. The smile never fading.

"Yes. Adam Parker," Becky said. "What about him?"

"Parker. Parker. Parker." Her smiles turned into giggles.

"Dammit." Becky said. The girl kept saying Adam's last name over and over. "Why do you want to kill him?"

The girl stopped. The giggling subsided.

"Adam Parker is next. He's going to learn his lesson. He's going to know what it feels like to lose everything."

"What? Why? How? Who are you?"

"Adam Parker is next. Adam Parker is next."

"Shit!" Becky shouted.

Someone cleared their throat from behind her. Becky slowly turned around to find all six officers and one police chief. Kenney glared at her. Kevin was in the grasp of the two Hilldale cops. He waved.

Becky waved back.

* * *

Once again, they were in the familiar surroundings of the Hilldale police station. Becky and Kevin sat in front of Kenney's desk, while the police chief was on the phone with the hospital about the 24-hour detail and how long it needed to be in effect. He shouted his final reply into the receiver before slamming it down on the base.

Then he turned his ire to Becky and Kevin.

"You heard what she said?" Becky didn't give Kenney the chance to yell.

He didn't yell. This time. "I did."

"And?"

"And that's why I placed two officers in front of Parker's home."

Kevin inched forward in the chair. "Chief. You can't think that this girl wants to kill Adam?"

"She's making the threats. She carved that threat into the wall of *Lonnie's* basement. I think that's a pretty good indicator of her intentions." Kenney tossed a file at Kevin. It landed on his lap.

"What's this?" Kevin asked.

"Her name. Kiley Conner. College student over at *Conn U.* You know, the place you burned down recently."

Becky shot to her feet. "That wasn't our fault!"

"Ms. Conner might disagree with you." Kenney leaned back in his chair. "Maybe she knew the kid that gave you that shiner. Gregory Bond."

She touched her eye upon mention of it. "That's impossible."

"Impossible that she knew him?" Kenney asked.

"That's not impossible," Kevin said. "But what's extremely unlikely is the connection between this girl and the murder of Fred Thompson. At least not directly."

Kenney scoffed. "How so?"

"The timeline. Fred died before the stuff with Bond ever went down. That doesn't make sense. She avenged Bond's capture before he was captured?"

"You were investigating Bond. She could've known Parker was close and decided to enact some early revenge," Kenney offered.

"And then go crazy and cause a scene at *Lonnie's*?" Becky asked, but it was rhetorical. "Yeah, that makes sense." She was being sarcastic, a staple of the Parker Agency.

"You work as a cop long enough, you see some pretty stupid things that even the smartest people do," Kenney said.

She placed her hands down on Kenney's desk and leaned in. "It's not her."

"She's the only lead we have right now. She's the only suspect in the Brookville murder. Kiley Conner may not be the killer, but she's the only thing we have connecting the Thompson murder and the threat on Parker." Kenney got up from behind his desk. "Adam Parker is next. He's going to learn a lesson. He's going to know what it feels like to lose everything. She said it. She wrote it. She's our best chance to finding out what's going on."

Becky and Kevin had no response. They looked to the ground. The office door shook from an officer knocking. The door opened, and the officer barked, "He's here."

Becky lifted her head. "Who's here?"

Kenney pointed over her shoulder. She turned to see her husband, Mark, who's face held a mix of anger and hurt that he couldn't hide.

# Chapter 11
## Taken

Adam stared out of the passenger window. He surveyed Hilldale's darkened suburban streets. Nancy sat quietly in the driver seat, texting on her cell phone. The soft clicks of her thumbs on the text keyboard were the only sounds inside the car. They had been parked for over ten minutes, in the same spot they first began their Brookville adventure.

"Seriously. Are you getting out?" Nancy finally broke the silence without looking up from the phone.

Adam kept his focus on the darkness. "Who are you texting?"

"Nun-ya."

He laughed and finally turned away from his thoughts. "Look. Just leave my name out of whatever it is you plan on doing with those other files you took from the Brookville Sheriff Station."

"We all have our little hobbies."

"You are a weird person, Nancy Olliver."

"We're all weird, Adam. Even you."

He nodded. "Even me." He grabbed the door handle. He pushed the door opened but paused before getting out. He was caught in a thought with one foot on the pavement.

Nancy groaned. "What now?"

He turned. Debating whether to ask. "Am I a bad guy?"

"What?"

"You have some pretty strong opinions of me. So, I'm asking. Am I one of the bad ones?"

She stopped texting. She glanced out the driver-side window, avoiding eye contact. An internal debate on whether she should lie or tell the truth. "Like bad in the sense of evil? No. I know you mean well. Plus, you and Kevin are tight. I see it. I get it. But you didn't used to be that way."

"High school was so long ago."

"For you. But not for some. People hold onto a lot of shit."

Adam finally stepped out of the car. Before shutting the door behind him, he leaned into the car. "You sure that cop won't remember us? The one you...whatevered."

"I'm sure."

He shrugged. "And you'll send me that file?"

"As soon as I get home."

He shut the door. He walked down his neighbor's driveway, returning to his house the way he snuck out. The car pulled away. Adam made quick work of the back hedges the other way around, which he wished Nancy had seen to make up for his disastrous first attempt.

Once back inside his house, he looked out the front window at his police protection. Still parked. Two shadows sitting in the front seat. Still no movement. Adam thought they might've fallen asleep.

He stared for a few minutes more. Their heads down. Motionless. In fact, they looked to be in the same position as when Adam left for Brookville. If he had to guess, Adam thought they looked exactly the same. A wave of concern brushed over him. A terrifying hunch that he needed to make sure wasn't true. He grabbed the front door handle., but before he pulled the door open he felt something in the room. A presence.

He wasn't alone. In the house. In the room. Behind him.

He spun around. *Whack!*

The back of his head stung with pain. He fell forward. Smacked his forehead on the door. He tried to regain his balance, but something was wrong. The room spun. His legs wobbled. He reached out for the edge of the couch to steady him. It wasn't enough. He lost his grip. He lost his footing. He fell. His face slapped the wooded floor boards.

A pair of shoes. Converse. Stood over him. The image blurred. He blinked his eyes, but the blurred image remained. Then it went black.

Adam passed out.

* * *

Mark steered the car onto their street. They passed the police car still parked in front of Adam's house. Becky made note of the two officers appearing to check their phones, heads down. Mark didn't bother to look, as he was still angry over the latest incident with Becky.

From the back seat, Kevin looked at Adam's house, hoping to see if he was home. He hadn't heard from Nancy or Adam yet, which didn't mean the planned break-in went bad, but it still caused Kevin to worry. He made a mental note to himself to text Nancy when he got home.

The car took a hard turn into the driveway and halted to a stop. Mark turned off the engine and bolted from the vehicle. Kevin pulled himself up and out from the backseat in time to see the front door shutting behind Mark as he entered the house. Becky waved a timid goodbye. She skulked to the front door. Kevin crossed the street towards his home. He glanced towards the police cruiser. Still no movement. His uneasiness grew.

Becky knew there was a fight on the other side of her front door, which was why she took her time walking to the house. The entire night was a bust and having Mark with a big "told you so" speech at the end of it wasn't what she needed right now. She closed the door behind her and Mark was nowhere to be found.

It was late, meaning the kids were already in their rooms and their beds, hopefully sleeping. From the kitchen, she heard the refrigerator door open and shut. She made her way there to find Mark pouring a glass of soda.

He stopped once Becky entered the room. He didn't turn around. "I'll sleep down here tonight."

"That's a slight overreaction, isn't it?" Becky asked.

Mark turned his head. "Is it?"

"I'd like to explain myself."

Mark twisted the cap shut on the soda bottle and turned around. "I'll explain it for you. You had to help Adam. He's in trouble. They need you."

"That's not fair."

"It's not, I know. But it's the truth. It's what I hear every week these days."

"Someone is trying to kill him, Mark."

"And you're standing next to him, so what do think that means? You're a target, too. After everything that happened four months ago, you run back into the fire." He wrenched the refrigerator door open and slammed the soda bottle on a shelf.

"Just. Listen to me. Please," Becky pleaded.

"What's to say? You'll do what you want."

"What I want is for us to not fight."

Mark slammed the refrigerator door shut. Anything on the shelves inside the door toppled over. "Then stop running around at night playing detective!"

"Or what?" Becky folded her arms. She leaned on the counter. "You won't be here when I come home?"

"No," he stormed out of the kitchen, "Or one night, you may not come home at all."

That stung Becky. She knew he was right. She was taking a lot of chances and with the new case, it didn't seem to be letting up. Was she willing to sacrifice her family for the rush of solving a case? Was it worth it? What was more important to her?

She found Mark in the living room. Planted on the couch, surfing through the channels. Not really paying attention to what was on the television.

Becky straddled him and brought her face right up to his. "I love you."

"I know."

"And I'll quit, I promise."

"But?"

"After this last case. It's too important."

"Until the next one," Mark arched his head to see the TV. Becky grabbed his face and pulled it back to her. She locked eyes with him.

"I love being a detective, but I love you and the kids more. I promise. This is it. No more late nights. No more stakeouts. No more shiners."

Mark reached up. He touched her eye. Careful not to hurt it. "It's a lovely shade of purple-yellow."

"I really should start putting make-up over it."

"Nah," Mark smiled. "Don't hide it. It's you."

They kiss. Deeply. Soon their hugging and holding each other. In that moment, alone in the house. They relax in an embrace and enjoy the presence of each other. Alone. Together. As one.

"Someone is really trying to kill Adam?" Mark asked.

"Yes. If I walk away now and they succeed, do you know how that will feel? The regret. The pain. I can't *not* do anything."

"Stop. I get it," he closed his eyes. Took a deep breath. "Please be safe."

They kissed again. They hugged. The tension released from the room.

Mark leaned back, "Why were you at the hospital tonight?"

"A Jane Doe the police discovered at *Lonnie's*. She was found writing a threat about Adam on the basement wall. Kenney thinks she's the key."

"But not you." Mark answered her doubts for her.

She shook her head. "It doesn't make any sense. She's in some bar talking about how Adam is next and how he's going to find out what it's like to lose everything. This is right after killing this guy in Brookville and leaving a note on a gravestone for him to see." Becky rambled on. "Why would you leave a note and then let yourself get caught in the basement of some dive?"

Mark feigned being hurt. "Hey. *Lonnie's* isn't a dive."

Becky planted a hard kiss on her husband's lips. "It holds a special place in my heart, too, but it's a dive."

"Yeah, I know." Mark smiled. The memories of their first encounter made his smile even bigger. Then he remembered something. "She was in the basement?"

"They found her down there. Apparently, she was there for a few days. She scratched the threat into the wall with her nail."

"That's creepy."

"Didn't smell great either."

"You know, back in the day, we would hang out in basement. The bartenders. It was where we would smoke when on break."

"I remember that. We went down there one time..." Becky smiled as she reminded him by reaching down his pants.

Mark laughed, after another long, this time softer, kiss. Becky pulled away. "Wait. Did it lead to the alley? Could you get to the alley from the window?"

"Not really," he shook his head. "Sometimes we'd open the window so we could get high down there without the owner realizing it."

"You never told me that!" Becky slapped him playfully on the chest.

"That was before I met you and maybe a little during."
Mark reached up with his right hand and rubbed the back of
Becky's neck. He brought the left hand up and cupped her
face, planning to bring it down for another kiss and maybe
more.

Becky stopped. "And the back door. It locks from the
inside."

"Yeah, why?" Mark dropped his hands. "Dammit. You're
onto something."

She nodded. "Give me ten minutes to make a call. Then
I'm going to bed and you better be in it waiting for me."
They kissed again.

* * *

Kevin went straight to his room when he came home. He
wanted to talk to Adam about their night at the hospital and,
of course, find out about the trip to Brookville, but Adam
wasn't answering his cell phone. This wasn't uncommon for
Adam. He'd often forget to charge his phone or even
remember where he left it. Kevin gave up being worried
about Adam missing his phone calls a long time ago. He
accepted his best friend's ineptitude when it came to any
form of communication.

What really troubled Kevin was the police cruiser parked
in front of Adam's house. Something wasn't right. He studied
the cruiser from his bedroom window and nothing changed.
The two officers never moved. It bothered all the way
through the late-night snack his mother prepared for him
when he came home.

The impromptu meal consisted of questions about the
case and Adam. Kevin and Adam were such good friends
growing up, that Adam was often joining the Simpsons for

most meals when they were younger. He was like a second son to the Kevin's parents.

It was natural for them to be worried. Kevin didn't blame his parents, but the constant questioning didn't really help with the enjoyment of his bagel bites or ease his concern about the motionless officers in the cruiser parked outside. Besides the fact, that Kevin was still confused about the girl at the hospital and what her message meant. Becky was right. It didn't make sense.

When he returned to his bedroom, Kevin surfed the internet for any kind of news that related to the Thompson murder in Brookville or the girl in the hospital. Nothing but standard news reports that revealed less than Kevin already knew.

But that cruiser. It still bothered him. *Why?*

His cell phone rang. He opened it up without looking at the caller ID.

"Adam!"

"No, it's me." Becky said over the phone.

"Sorry. Have you heard from him?"

"No. We just got back. They still might be doing the thing." Becky didn't want to reveal too much. "That's not why I called."

"What's up?"

"The Jane Doe."

"I thought we don't like her for the Thompson murder."

"I don't, but that doesn't mean she wasn't involved."

"I'm confused."

"Maybe she knew whoever killed Fred Thompson. We agree she was in the basement for some time."

"Yes. Gross. Don't remind me about the pile." Kevin shook his head, trying to erase the memory of what he saw in that basement.

"There's a window in the basement, but it's not big enough for anyone to get through. The back door that leads to the alley only locks from the inside." Becky worked out her theory aloud over the phone.

"What are you saying?" Kevin asked.

She stopped. The line was quiet. "I'm not sure. But, there's no way for anyone to get in that basement without going through the front door."

"Unless someone lets them in through the back door."

"Yeah," Becky trailed off. "I don't know. It feels like we missed something."

Kevin looked out his window again. "Did you notice the cops outside?"

"What about them?"

He paused. Contemplating his own paranoia. "It's probably nothing. Never mind."

"You sure?" Becky asked.

"Yeah. We'll talk about your Jane Doer theory tomorrow. Night, Beck."

Kevin hung up and returned to his computer. He surfed through his *Facebook* feed, seeing what his friends were up to with their lives. He quickly grew tired of it. The police cruiser still on his mind.

He returned to the window. Stared at the cruiser. He didn't know what was bothering him so much about it, but it wasn't going away. What did he say to himself at dinner? *Motionless.*

He smacked his window with the palm of his hand. He decided his next course of action. He charged out of his room. He shoved the front door with such force that the door smacked into the side of the house. Loud. He stopped. Looked to the police cruiser to see if the noise sparked any reaction from Adam's protection detail. Still nothing.

"What the hell?" Kevin said aloud.

He made his way across the street. As he got closer to the car, he waved a 'hello', not wanting to get yelled at or shot.

The officer on the driver side said nothing. His head was straight down.

Kevin was close enough to the car now that they couldn't ignore him. "Hey. You guys hungry or something?" It seemed like a good reason to come over.

No response.

Kevin leaned on the window. It was open. He bent down for a better look. "You guys both sleeping?"

A sense of dread struck Kevin in his gut. The warmth of awfulness rose up his spine and raised the hairs on the back of his neck. He reached into the car and placed his hand on the officer's shoulder. He shook it.

The head wobbled forward and then back, revealing a long slit along the throat. The wound had been opened quite some time ago as the blood no longer flowed but congealed. Kevin turned away. The smell hit him. He recoiled, holding back the urge to vomit.

# Chapter 12
## Same Pants

He was still home. The living room was dark. It was night. The lights were off. Adam lay on the floor. His breathing was shallow. Then, he was lifted up. He floated through the room into the kitchen. Out the opened back door. Down the concrete steps and into the driveway. He floated alongside a car. The trunk was open. And then, complete blackout.

It felt like a dream, but Adam sensed it wasn't his imagination. Pieces of time he experienced. While it was pitch black inside the trunk, he could hear outside the car. He could smell the outside air. Tires over asphalt. The trunk heaved with each pothole. The smell of trees, which isn't uncommon for Hilldale. Sounds of the car gave way to rushing water. A river or a stream. Perhaps, a brook. Then nothing. Blackness.

He was wet. His neck first. Cold. It soaked his shirt, down his back. Another splash of water. Adam awoke. Water rushed down his throat. He choked it back up. A bucket bounced on the floor next to him. Adam was soaked from his shirt to his sneakers.

Adam tried to wipe his face, but his arms couldn't move. They were tied behind his back, around a metal, fold-up chair. The room was lit from an overhead chandelier made from deer antlers. He looked to the wall and heads of animals looked back. Black, plastic orbs where their eyes once were.

Adam was in a hunting cabin.

"I got tired of waiting for you to wake up."

A man stood firm in front of Adam. Black converse sneakers, slightly scuffed, black pants and a sweatshirt. Black as well. Adam couldn't make out the mysterious man's face. Water still blurred his vision.

Adam coughed. "Floor's wet."

"Always a smart ass," the man said. He stepped into the light. Adam made out the long, stringy hair that came to a rest at the base of the man's neck. His face pock-marked from years of acne. His nose slightly hooked, and his eyes could be called beady by some.

"People will come looking for me," Adam said.

The man quietly shushed him, "Now, now. Let's not play pretend. No one is going to find you. Not now." He took position behind Adam, his hands on Adam's shoulders.

"Why not?"

"Because no one saw me take you."

"What about the two cops stationed outside the house?"

"No longer in existence," he said through a toothy grin.

Adam knew what he meant. "That's some dark stuff, right there"

"It's going to get darker."

"How so? How am I going to die?"

"After I'm finished doing everything I want."

"Who are you?"

Another smile. "All in good time, Adam Parker."

The man walked around Adam, grabbing another metal chair. He unfolded it and placed it in front of Adam. Face to face. He sat down. The man took a good long look and allowed Adam to do the same.

The pock-marked face. The dark, stringy hair. Dark, hazel eyes. Wrinkles along the brow. Adam had no idea who was grinning back at him.

"I don't understand," Adam said.

"You don't know who I am, do you?"

"Should I?"

"If you want to survive all of this. Yes, you should."

Adam eased up. He leaned back. "You wrote the note."

The man snapped his fingers. "Bingo was his name-o. I was hoping you'd see that gravestone. I almost spray-painted all of the gravestones, just to be certain."

"Seriously, who are you?"

"I'll give you a hint." The man moved fast. He delivered a right cross to Adam's nose, which caused his head to jerk back. Blood instantly leaked from his nose. Adam moaned.

"What kind of hint was that?" Adam asked. He blinked his eyes a few times to clear out the cobwebs.

"Sorry. I lied. I just wanted to do that."

Adam figured a snarky retort wouldn't go over well, so he opted for silence. The man stood up and walked towards a large window that looked out over the darkened skyline littered with treetops. Adam couldn't place the view, just that there were a lot of trees.

Without turning from the window, the man spoke, "You are Adam Parker. Class of Hilldale 1999, yes?"

"Haven't we established this already?"

The man smiled. "We're going to take a trip down memory lane and you're going to learn what type of person you really are."

"So, we're playing a game of some sort? I solve some clues, until what? I win, and you go to jail. I mean, why not just skip to the end?"

"Careful." The man pulled a gun from his waistband. He stepped closer. Pressed the barrel to Adam's forehead.

Adam flinched. "All right. I get it."

"Do you?" He pushed the barrel harder, making an indent in Adam's forehead.

"Ok, ok. What's this game you're talking about?"

The man eased back. Gun placed back in his waistband. "The rules are simple. I will give you your first clue and that will lead you to a location. Once you realize why you're there, a new clue will make itself known and this will continue on and on."

"Until?"

He reached down and grabbed Adam's shirt. Pulled him close to his face, "Until you understand the monster that you are." He shoved Adam back. A few deep breaths and returned to his chair. All the while, keeping his head down. Controlling the anger that boiled under the surface.

Adam sensed a rage-fueled explosion could be imminent. "Dude. Seriously? Who the hell are you?"

He raised his head. Slowly. He stared at Adam. Piercing. "You really don't know, do you?"

"What tipped you off?" Adam asked. He smirked.

The man brought his head forward, connecting with Adam's face. Blood no longer leaked from his nose, it poured. He winced from the pain.

"Do you ever stop being a smart-ass?" The man asked. "I mean, at some point, you do realize it's pointless to be this dumb, right?"

Adam had no response. He tried wiping his bloody nose on his shoulder but couldn't reach. The man leaned back in his chair. Crossed his legs. Took a deep breath and let out:

"My name is Oliver Francis."

\* \* \*

During Adam's senior year at Hilldale High, he was usually dropped off early at school by his mother when she was on her way to work. They only owned the one car. While he enjoyed the fruits of being popular in school, Adam still suffered the indignity of not having his own vehicle. It was just him and his mother for most of his childhood. The money that would've gone to a beat-up, old car for Adam was needed for food, the mortgage and other more pressing needs.

He understood. He never complained. His only problem was the early drop-off time. Adam often found himself in school an hour before first bell. His mother worked early which meant he had to get ready for school early, which made for more than the average grumpy mornings at the Parker household.

Most school mornings he spent in front of his locker on the third floor. His routine was almost the same – get dropped off by the front entrance, head downstairs, grab an egg sandwich from the cafeteria and then straight to his locker where he would enjoy his breakfast and finish up some homework.

Not many people bothered him on the third floor. It was nice and quiet, a welcome comparison to the chaos that is high school. His partner in crime for these mornings became one of his best friends during senior year of school, Fred Thompson.

Fred was on Hilldale High's track and field team. For the first three years of school, he spread his talents over several events with the team. But when senior year started, Fred made the commitment to cross-country running, which required the early morning practice sessions. He came to school early for these practices, but had twenty-minutes before they started, so he took that time to also enjoy his breakfast at his locker. It just happened that his locker was two down from Adam.

That first week of senior year, Fred and Adam talked sports, school and girls, not all in that order. Fred was rail thin, like most runners. He was taller than Adam, just topping out at six feet, two inches. His pale skin and red hair revealed his Irish roots and also made him stand out in a crowded hallway during a class change. That's usually how Adam saw him throughout the day. Fred's red hair bopping along a few inches higher than the rest of Hilldale High's student body.

They'd merely nod to each other throughout the day. In fact, most of their interactions during a school day took place during that twenty minutes of locker breakfast every morning. Each of them ran with different social circles, so they never figured out how to connect on the weekends. Plus, they were teenagers, notorious for poor time-management skills.

After that first week of school, they were visited by another student. This one was not a senior. Freshman, class of 2003. He was small. His black hair spiked a bit from styling gel. He was unassuming, not looking to make an impression. At first, Adam and Fred paid him no mind. He went to his locker, got his books and then left. It took five minutes. His name was Oliver Francis.

But back then, Adam and Fred never knew his name. They really didn't think anything about the freshman until the third week of school, when Adam noticed a theme with Oliver's appearance. At first, Adam thought he was imagining it, but on that Tuesday of the third week when Oliver showed up for school at his locker, Adam couldn't help but pry.

"Hey. Didn't you wear those pants last week?" The question took Fred by surprise. He looked up expecting Adam to be staring at him, but instead Adam's gaze was across the hallway.

The small, freshman with the spiky hair darted his eyes to the floor.

Oliver said nothing. He quietly walked to his locker, turning his back on the two tormentors.

Fred chimed in, picking up on Adam's suspicion. "Seriously. You wore that same pair all last week."

"It's cool, you know," Adam continued, "I think it takes a lot of guts to wear the same pants all week long."

"You got guts, son?" Fred said in a southern, general-like voice.

They laughed. Oliver remained silent. He fidgeted with the combination on the locker. His hands shook with from nerves.

"C'mon, man. Don't get quiet. Are those the same pants as last week?"

"The whole of last week," Fred added.

He gave up on the lock and headed out the way he entered. He didn't care if his books for first period remained inside the locker. He'd get them later. Oliver hurried his pace.

Adam called out. "Same Pants! Don't leave! We need to know!"

And the name - Same Pants - was born. Every morning, Adam and Fred enjoyed their breakfast and waited for Same Pants to enter the hallway wearing the exact same pants as he did the day before. They'd tease him as Oliver got ready for school from his locker. They wouldn't let up. Ever. At one point, the idea of bullying came up, but they were seventeen years old and having fun. They didn't care.

This continued for most of the year. If Adam or Fred missed a day of school, the other would ask whether or not Same Pants showed up with same pants. He did. He always did. Every day. All year long. And they were there to make fun of him every single morning.

* * *

Adam said nothing. The information about his captor still processing in his mind. Francis moved to the window again. He studied the tree-tops. He noticed no movement. No wind. He wondered if Adam took notice of that as well. He slightly turned his head and spotted Adam out of the corner of this eye. He was glaring at the floor. Francis waited for a response.

"That was sixteen years ago," Adam said.

"But you remember it now, don't you?" Francis didn't fully turn away from the window. He folded his hands behind his back.

"Sure. Yeah, but I was a teenager. I was dumb."

"You were having fun. Fun at the expense of me. Of my feelings."

"You think you're the first freshman that's ever been picked on in the history of high school? Give me a break!"

Francis spun around. He charged at Adam. "Every morning that year I woke up with dread. I wanted nothing to do with school. I didn't want to go to my locker. Some days, I'd wait for you to leave before getting my things, which usually meant I was late for class. But I didn't care. I didn't want to have to listen to that...that...name!"

"It was just in good fun. There are far worse things we could've done and said to you. Believe me."

Francis laughed. "I've tied you up. Pointed a gun to your head. And your tactic is to have me thank you for not torturing me more than you could've back then?"

"I'm just saying..."

"No!" Francis cut him off. "You don't get to say anything. Adam Parker. Popular kid in school that made everyone laugh. Always there for a verbal jab at an unsuspecting kid in the hallway. You may have been one of the "cool kids", but you were never liked by people like me."

"Freshman?"

Francis slugged him again. This time across the face, hammering the side of his eye. Adam cursed from the pain.

"People who you considered less than. People not cool enough to hang with you. You were feared. Hated."

"Look. I'm sorry. I'm sorry for what we called you."

"Gee. Thanks. That makes me feel better now." Francis clapped his hands. "You know what? I'm sorry. Let me untie you." Adam forced a smiled, even though he wasn't thrilled with the sarcasm.

Francis inched closer. "You ready to play our game?"

"Why? What's the point?"

"The game. The game is the point. Play it and survive."

"What about Fred? He didn't get a choice, did he?"

"Fred was a lackey. He was your sidekick and besides I needed to get your attention."

"Friend me on Facebook then!" Adam shot back.

Francis delivered yet another blow, this one to Adam's stomach. Adam doubled over from the pain. Francis knelt down. He was close to Adam. He whispered into Adam's ear. "You should be thanking me. I could've killed someone closer to you. Maybe your girlfriend with the husband. Maybe I should've ran her through with my 3-iron."

Adam stomped the floor with his foot, even though it was still tied to the chair. He stomped again. And again. He screamed "I don't want to play this stupid game!"

Francis laughed. "You don't have a choice, Parker."

Adam had a ridiculous thought. He regained his breath from the gut punch. He sat up. Face to face with Francis. "Actually, I do. The point of this game is to make me suffer, right? To make me feel like a piece of shit. But if I refuse, you'll just kill me. If you kill me, then you can't make me suffer from all the pain I've caused. So, you're stuck."

Francis smiled. "I'm glad you got there."

"Realizing the flaw in your plan? Thanks, I guess."

Francis walked towards a closet door. He leaned against the wall next to it. "When I first came up with this idea, I figured that might be an issue."

"And yet, you went through with it." Adam shook his head. "Not smart."

"No, but this was." Francis grabbed the closet door handle and pulled it open. Tied to another chair was Kevin. A gag taped in his mouth. He looked at Adam, then to Francis. Confusion all over his face.

Adam jerked in his chair. "No!"

"Yes!" Francis pulled the gun out again. He cocked the hammer and jammed the barrel into the side of Kevin's head.

Kevin screamed through the gag in his mouth.

"This is about me! Not Kevin."

"You really are naïve. But don't worry, you'll figure it out. So, looks like you don't have a choice but to play my game or Kevin here, dies."

Adam looked to his friend. "I'm going to stop him. I swear. I'll make him pay." He turned his rage to Francis. "Now what?"

"That was really sweet what you just said. Inaccurate, but sweet. You play the game until the end or Kevin dies. You come for me before the game is over, Kevin dies."

"Let me guess. If I tell the cops, Kevin dies?" Adam's attempt at humor was to mask his nervousness.

"Tell whoever you like. They can't save Kevin. Only one person can do that."

Adam's eyes watered. Emotion got the better of him. He looked to ground, avoiding eye contact with Francis. "Tell me where to start."

"Let the game begin."

Francis walked towards Adam. He flipped the gun around in his hand, handle out. He brought the butt of the gun hard down on the back of Adam's neck and head, knocking him out cold.

# Chapter 13
## It Begins

Becky made a point to wake up early this morning. She wanted to make a big breakfast, the kind she used to make before the Parker Agency came back into her life. Eggs, bacon and toast were on the menu although Jake wanted cereal and Becky learned a long time ago that it was easier to just pour the bowl of cereal rather than force-feed eggs to her son.

In fact, Jake never wanted anything that was made for him. Not matter the meal, Jake wanted something else. Sandwich? Nope. He wanted pasta. Pasta? Jake chose a sandwich. It was a lose-lose scenario for Becky and Mark. It took weeks of tantrums and empty threats of punishment before the ultimate policy of appeasement was enacted. All the parenting books tell you to stand firm, but Becky was certain the authors of those books never had strong-willed children.

Caitlyn didn't speak when she entered the kitchen, which was the norm. Teenage angst being what it is these days, Caitlyn's feelings were better expressed with emojis through texts. Becky had deeper, more meaningful conversations with her daughter through their phones than they ever did around the kitchen table.

Mark was last to come down for breakfast. In a rush to get to the office, he grabbed a piece of buttered toast from the table and made for the front door. Becky grabbed his collar and pulled him tight. "Not without this, you don't."

They kissed. Groans came from the table. Jake and Caitlyn were equally displeased with their parents' public display of affection.

"Get over it," Becky chirped back. "How do you think you got here?"

"Ew, Mom! C'mon!" Caitlyn understood her mother's subtext.

"How'd we get where?" Jake did not.

Mark said his goodbyes before racing out of the kitchen. Becky heard the front door shut behind him, as she returned to the sink. The breakfast meal clean-up commenced. She heard the front door open again. Mark entered the kitchen.

Becky spun around. "Back for seconds?"

Mark wasn't smiling. She could tell he was nervous.

"What is it?"

* * *

The neighborhood was loaded with police officers. Pockets of uniformed men were scattered across the road. Police cruisers blocked the street at the bottom of the hill, while barricades were set up just beyond Becky's driveway. A few officers went door to door, looking for answers.

Becky stood at the top of her front steps, taking it all in, not sure how to proceed. Without realizing it, she was down the steps and walking towards the roped off cruiser. The same one that was parked in front of Adam's house all night. A large collection of police was around the car. She still had the dish towel in her hand. She stopped on her front lawn, when she spotted Kenney barking orders to several officers. Mark came up behind her.

Mark placed his hand on her shoulder. "I know you have to go over there."

"Something is wrong, Mark. That's the detail assigned to watch Adam."

"You think he's..." Mark didn't finish his thought aloud.

Becky turned to him. "Listen. I meant everything I said last night. But I need to find out what's going on and if that leads to..."

Mark stopped her with a kiss. He smiled. "Go do what you need to do."

She smiled, tossed the dish towel onto the lawn and headed straight for Kenney. He spotted Becky heading his way and broke off from his conversation to meet her in the street.

"What's going on?" She tried to hide her nerves.

"I've got two officers dead."

She cupped her hands to her mouth. "Adam?"

"Not home, but that doesn't mean anything. I'm not stupid enough to think he wouldn't try to leave the house. If you and Simpson were out causing trouble last night, I suspect Adam was as well."

"That doesn't explain your officers."

Kenney sighed. "No, it doesn't." Kenney took a moment to survey the street and all its activity. "So, where is he?"

\* \* \*

He had a massive headache. Face flat on the ground. Dirt shoved into his mouth and up his nose. The whir of lawn mowers roused him from his unconscious state. He repeatedly blinked his eyes hoping to find their focus. What he saw was the ground. Slanted. He took a few breaths and inhaled more dirt, immediately coughing it back out. He forced himself up to a seated position. He rubbed his eyes with the palms of his hands. His head still pounding.

The lawn mowers were still running. Adam followed their 4-cycle engine sounds to across the road. A tall, grassy field was being groomed by several manned mowers. The landscaping crew made quick work of the tall grass. None of them paid mind to the young man staring at them in groggy haze from across the street.

He stood up. His head was spinning. He reached out his hand and found a large wooden structure to rest his hand on. He balanced himself to prevent crashing back down to the ground. The bright, morning sun forced his eyes shut, which worsened his condition. The dizziness intensified. His head pounded. He gripped the flat panel of wood. Pieces of paint scraped under his fingernails.

A car flew by. It startled him. He lost his grip. He stumbled, smacking his back against the wood panel. *Thud!* He maintained his balance. He rested for a bit, taking a few deep breaths before trying to move again. He leaned back on the wood structure currently keeping him upright. He regained his balance. The dizziness subsided. He stepped forward and turned around to see what had kept him upright.

The *'Welcome to Hilldale'* sign looked back at him. One of a few that sat on the outskirts of the town. Usually donated by a local business. Adam spun back to the road to ascertain his surroundings. He glanced up and down the road. He knew where he was now. Another throbbing jolt of pain from behind his right eye. His headache was now a migraine. He rubbed the side of his head to alleviate the pain, anything to make the long walk back home manageable.

The migraine intensified. Adam rubbed his head harder. He took several steps and suddenly was on the ground again. The vertigo returned. Disoriented. The lawn mowers stopped. Voices called out.

Adam's vision blurred. The migraine engulfed his whole head. A warmness seeped to his neck. He put his hand on his neck. Hoping to rub the ache away. He didn't make it. He passed out.

* * *

It was odd being back to the hospital after just being arrested for being there the night before. Becky felt the stares from the nurses and doctors who recognized her from last night's incident. She expected someone to ask her to leave. Any moment security would charge around the corner. The fear was real, but quickly dissipated once Kenney spotted her. He waved her down the hallway. She half-smiled and joined him.

After the discovery in front of Adam's home that morning, Becky tried to find something to occupy her time and her mind. She called Kevin, but his cell phone went straight to voice mail. Not unusual for him to sleep late, even though she expected him to be outside with all the commotion on the street. With the officers going door to door, she figured they'd ask to speak with Kevin knowing his relationship with Adam. But no. He wasn't around. And now, as she called his cell phone. He wasn't answering. It bothered her.

She stood at the front window, debating about walking across the street to wake up Kevin. It had to be done, she thought. She grabbed her front door handle when the phone rang. It was Kenney. They found Adam.

This is what brought her back to the hospital. She jogged down the hallway. Kenney held up his hand to stop her. "He was out on Route 34. Couple of landscapers found him passed out along the side of the road."

"How'd he get out there?"

"I need to know what he was up to, Ms. Clarkson." Kenney wasn't playing around. "I need to know now."

She sighed. "Brookville. He was looking into the Thompson murder. He thought there might be a clue to who was after him."

"Where in Brookville?"

She skirted her eyes to the side. "Well, you know when there's a murder, there's an investigation and notes are taken..."

"Jesus," Kenney rubbed his face. He knew where Adam was last night, "If he wasn't in that room, I'd no doubt put him in there myself. Are you kidding me?"

"I know. I know." Becky professed.

"Dammit!" Kenney's anger wasn't subsiding. "You can't be breaking into..." He looked around and pulled Becky further down the hallway, away from the hospital room. "You just can't do this kind of stuff."

"Chief. Someone wants to kill Adam." She held his gaze. "We need to find out who and sometimes we may need to do things that aren't...you know...legit."

"Breaking the law will get you locked up. That won't help him."

"It wasn't me who did whatever it is you think Adam did in Brookville," she dodged implicating herself nicely. "We're just trying to find out who wants him dead."

From the room, a voice called out, "Maybe if you stop talking out in the hall and come in here, I'll tell you."

They found Adam sitting up in his hospital bed. He sipped from a small, plastic juice cup. "See if there are any more of these in the hall, will ya?"

"Later," Kenney walked to one side of the bed. "What happened?"

"So, no more apple juice?"

Becky stood at the foot of the bed. "Adam. This is serious."

"I know." He sighed before revealing, "He has Kevin."

"What?" Kenney asked. "Who?"

"Oliver Francis," Adam started out. He relayed the events of the night. Being taken from his house. The cabin. The story of Same Pants. The revelation of the game he must play and what was at stake. Kevin's life.

After finishing the story, Adam procured another apple juice from a nurse who was checking his vitals. Becky took a seat in the corner during the story. The wave of information was overwhelming. Kenney remained stoic, taking in all the facts. At one point during Adam's story he produced a notebook and wrote a few thoughts down.

"Do you remember anything about the cabin?" Kenney asked.

"Not much. Antler chandelier. Animal heads on the wall. Smelled like the forest or tree, maybe. I didn't see much of outside. There was a stream somewhere outside."

"I might have some ideas as to where he took you," Kenney pulled out his phone. Sent a text.

"What're we going to do?" Becky asked, finally processing the information.

Kenney finished off his text and pocketed his phone. "Well, I'm going to contact Kevin's parents. Then I'm directing my men to find this cabin where Adam was held. Odds are Kevin is still there unless this Francis guy moved him." He looked to Adam, "You really bully this kid like he said?"

"It was high school. Who didn't get bullied?"

"Bullies," Becky replied.

He let the comment sink in. After his night, it stung. He looked back to Kenney. "Francis probably has some kind of reason to not like me, but to kill over it? I don't think it was that serious."

"Who are you to determine if it's serous or not?" Becky added. "If this kid felt tortured by you and your comments, even if you weren't being intentional malicious, it's a big issue."

"What am I supposed to do about it now, Becky?" Adam asked. "This was over fifteen years ago."

"Well, right now," Becky choked back her anger. "We need to rescue Kevin."

"We also need to tell her," Adam said.

Becky knew he meant Nancy. "Shit."

"Who?" Kenney asked.

"Kevin's girlfriend," Becky replied.

He paused. Shock ran across this face. "Seriously? Simpson has a girl?"

"Something like that," Adam said.

Kenney smiled. Proud of Kevin. "Good for him." He changed gears. "All right, I've got some work to do. Francis killed two of my guys. We're going to find him."

"And if you can't?" Adam asked.

"Then maybe you should play his game," Kenney paused. "But I never said that." He left the room but held up. He turned back. "What did you find out in Brookville?"

"Nothing of note. Just that the weapon was a 3-iron. The head came off to reveal a sharpened spear of some sort. He ran Fred through. Almost sixteen times."

"That's some anger," Kenney said.

"Directed at you, Adam," Becky said.

"I'm sorry. I have to get to work." Kenney left the room.

Once the door shut behind him, Becky turned to Adam, "Was he okay? Kevin."

"He looked scared, but not hurt."

She bowed her head quickly. Once. Believing Adam's assessment and accepting it as fact. "So, we play the game?"

"Something like that." Adam pulled the covers from the bed. His legs poked out of the generic hospital gown. He swung them over the side.

"Right now?"

"You heard Kenney. He has work to do and so do we. We don't have time to wait."

"Where are we supposed to start?"

Adam took a moment before standing. "That's what I've been trying to figure out. Francis told me each location would require me to remember its significance in order to discover the next clue."

"But where?" Becky asked.

"Where the game began. At the location he left me." He stood up and reached for his pants on the chair. He fell to the ground. His legs were still asleep. "I'm good. I'm good."

\* \* \*

Adam paced in a circle around the familiar '*Welcome to Hilldale*' sign from the morning. He was quiet. Deep in thought. Looking for clues. He knelt by the spot where he woke up. The drool stain was still damp. The landscaping crew had moved on to the other side of the field. They had their work cut out for them today.

Becky leaned on her mini-van which she parked along the side of the road. The occasional car horn would sound as people driving by knew Becky from various school activities and PTO events. She smiled with every car horn.

"I don't see it," Adam finally said.

"What're you looking for?"

"A note. A taped envelope. I don't know. Something."

"Maybes something happened here? In high school," Becky suggested.

"Honestly, I can't remember. I couldn't even recognize Francis."

"That's not surprising. It's not like he was your friend back then. You didn't hang out with him."

"But I had such an impact on his life, you'd think I remember," he added. A tinge of sarcasm included.

She paused. Dropped her head to his chest to gather her thoughts. "Gloria Keener."

"What'd I do to her?"

"Nothing. She was in my grade. She was into everything sports. Played soccer, basketball and ran track. Big girl, not heavy, but just strong," Becky shifted her spot on the mini-van. She stood upright. "Beginning of the school year, she had dropped her books in the middle of the hallway and when she picked them up, her pants split right down the middle. Everyone in the hallway laughed. I laughed. It was funny. Even Gloria was laughing."

"So, what happened? You found her crying that day and you felt so bad?" Adam was confident he knew the moral of the story.

Becky shook her head. "No, idiot. End of the school year. Me and Gloria end up at the same table for some kind of school fundraising thing. She tells me that she's never liked me since that day."

"Because you laughed?"

"She always thought I was nice, but when she me laughing at her, it just changed. Her perception of me changed all from seeing me laugh at her for five seconds."

"Kind of an overreaction, don't you think?" Adam scoffed.

She ignored Adam. "When she first told me, I thought she was being ridiculous. I told her to relax or something like that. But the next morning, I woke up feeling like such a jerk. I was so angry and upset. So, when I saw her the next day, I apologized."

"And you've been friends ever since. How lovely," Adam smiled, but it faded fast. "This isn't that. This is some psycho trying to teach me a stupid lesson by threating to kill my friend."

"My point is that even if you think you didn't do anything to Francis, no matter how small your impact, it's different on his end. You may have been teasing him, but it could've been torture for him." Becky's voice was raised. "And this 'psycho' is the way he is because of you."

"The jury is still out on that," Adam shot back.

"All I'm saying is that even though you may think you did nothing, to Francis you did enough to make him hate you."

Adam opened his mouth to retort, but an idea struck him. He turned to face the sign again. He read it aloud. "Welcome to Hilldale."

"Good talk," Becky tossed her hands up, giving up.

"It was. Something small can be big. I heard you."

"It wasn't about the sign," she added.

"But it is. The whole reason I was left here is about the sign. Our first clue." He stepped close to the sign, running his hands along the face of it. The sign listed the population: *24,892* (as of three years ago) Various organizations like the Elks Lodge and Friars Club were represented with their official seals.

"What are you looking for?" Becky asked.

Adam smiled. He rubbed his hand over the bottom of the sign. It read: *Sponsored by Slammin' Sushi.* He turned to Becky, "Hungry?"

# Chapter 14
## Tanaka-Bomb

The over-sized shrimp attached to the roof of the *Slammin Sushi* casted a large shadow over the sidewalk in front of the restaurant. Adam and Becky stood in the middle of the shadow as they peered through the darkened windows of the front doors. They had knocked several times and received no response. Becky, cell phone to her ear, heard the phone ringing from inside the restaurant.

"There's a car in the parking lot. I know someone is in there," Adam said.

She hung up the phone. Placed it back in her pocket. "Does anything about this place remind you of something from your high school days?"

"Nothing. This used to be video store. Hilldale Video."

"It was a Blockbuster."

"Don't think so. Hilldale Video. Blockbuster was in South Haven," Adam corrected her.

"You're wrong. As usual," she countered.

"I don't want to embarrass you, so just call again. I swear I saw someone move in there before," Adam said.

"Maybe they're not open. Sometimes, it's better to ignore customers than explain that they're not open."

"That's rude. What if they're not answering because they have Kevin tied up and they're torturing him?"

"First of all, my example is a bit more plausible and second, why would Francis set up this elaborate scavenger hunt of your past indiscretions, by holding Kevin hostage to make sure you do this, and the first place he sends you is where he's keeping Kevin?"

"It's not the craziest thing to believe. People are weird," Adam said.

*Squeal!* They spun around to find a red corvette parked awkwardly on the curb. The driver was already out of the car. Baseball bat in hand. He pointed with it at Adam. "What do you want?"

Adam raised his hands up. "Sushi?"

"We're closed." The man was Asian. His jet-black hair was not combed, and his clothes looked like they were scraped up from the floor. Silk shirt, wrinkled and black pants, also wrinkled.

"We're not looking for trouble," Becky held her hand up as well. "Just looking to talk with someone."

"What about?" His breath slowed. He rubbed his eyes. They were still glassy.

Adam took a chance. "You worked last night?"

"What?"

"You were the chef last night, right?"

He didn't know how to respond. He nodded.

Adam continued, "They wake you up? Told you we were out here knocking on the door and calling?"

"Yeah. Why do you think I'm here?"

"I think you're here because we scared someone in there. Probably an older person. Grandfather? Father? They called all upset, which is why you you're waving that bat around."

"It's my uncle. He gets spooked sometimes," he lowered the bat, "And if I was going to use this bat on you, I would've done it a long time ago, Parker." He pulled keys from his pocket. He unlocked the front door and entered leaving a stunned Adam, still holding his hands up.

Becky's head swiveled to Adam. He flipped his palms up, not knowing how to explain what just happened. She shook her head and left him alone on the sidewalk as she joined the man with the bat.

The restaurant was dark. Not only were the windows tinted, but the blinds were pulled shut. No morning sun was allowed entry into the dining area. As The smell of butter and cooked fish struck Adam as he walked through the restaurant. He found Becky standing alone by the bar. In the corner of the main room was a giant fish tank. Several large blue-gray colored fish calmly swam back and forth. Adam wondered if they were ambience or a dinner option.

An older, Asian man came out from the kitchen. The younger man, bat still in hand, was with him. The older man was mumbling. He was still scared. He held out his hands and cupped the younger man's face. They spoke another language, one that Adam didn't understand and only guessed it to be Japanese. Several pointed fingers were directed at Adam and Becky, before the older man returned to the kitchen.

"Do I know you?" Adam asked.

The man laughed. "Jesus. It has been a while, I'll give you that, but I don't think I changed that much."

"Who are you?" Becky asked.

The man held out his hand, "Please. Sit. My uncle is preparing some food for us. It's not really an option. Kind of a hospitality thing."

"You're still holding the bat," Adam pointed out.

"I am. Yes. Sorry about that." He propped the bat against the wall. He took a seat at a table and invited Becky and Adam to join him, which they did. "You really don't know, huh?"

Adam shook his head.

"Jeff Tanaka."

Adam's face froze. Becky noticed his demeanor change. "What? What is it?"

"He remembers me now," Tanaka said.

"Shit," Adam said.

"Shit?" Becky mimicked him. "What do you mean, 'shit'?"

Adam ignored her question. Stared straight at Tanaka, frozen in indecision. He wanted to say something. Anything. Any words seemed pointless.

Becky slapped the table. "Adam Parker. You tell me what's going on."

Tanaka smiled, but it wasn't out of joy. The memories were not good. "Tell you what. I'm going to help my uncle in the kitchen. Parker, why don't you fill in your friend about me? Then we can get back to figuring out why you're here."

Adam nodded. Tanaka smiled as he stood up from the table. He returned to the kitchen. As soon as the door swung shut, Becky grabbed Adam by the arm. "Tell me."

Adam sighed. "Jeff was in my class in high school. He was an okay, dude. Kept to himself." He paused. "You were already gone from school, so you probably didn't know him. He had a nickname in high school. A nickname I gave him."

"What'd you do?"

He took a deep breath, hoping his initial memory of the events were worse than they actually were, but the more he thought about it, the more the story scared him. Scared about who he was and the reaction he was about to get when he told Becky about Tanaka-Bomb.

* * *

The party was epic. This was the type of party you saw in the movies. It seemed like everyone who went to Hilldale High School between the years 1997-2001 were at this party. College kids, years removed from graduation showed up to the party. Even Middle schoolers, who thought they were cool enough, braved the possibility of ridicule to go to the party. It was the perfect mix of Hilldale's past, present and future.

Adam organized the party with a few other senior class members, but the true host was a sophomore. Justin Mathis. A rich kid who got everything he wanted from his parents except what they couldn't give him. Popularity. He revealed his desire to be popular with Adam one day after school, when they were stuck in the principal's office for separate issues. Once Adam found out that Mathis' parents were going to be out of town on the weekend, he capitalized on Mathis's need to be popular and convinced him to throw a huge party.

Mathis figured it'd only be a few upperclassmen, but with Adam's promotion, the party became much more. Droves of kids showed up at the front door, many from neighboring towns. Mathis spent most of the night in his own pool shed. Passed out from too many beers and tossed aside once he puked all over the would-be prom queen. The outcome was not what he intended, nor did he remember most of it.

Adam was in charge of the entertainment for the party. He secured the D.J. and a few inflatable bouncy houses that decorated the backyard. He also bought two kiddie pools. Adam filled each pool with mud and desired to have several of the girls in his class wrestle. He saw it in a movie when he was a kid and he always wanted to try it, since it usually ended with the girl and guy having sex. These were movies Adam watched in the privacy of his own bedroom and of course, he thought he could duplicate the same results.

But Adam wasn't done. He recently attended a school event where a member of a local circus performed for students and faculty. A fire-eater. He dazzled with placing various sticks of fire in his mouth, even blowing fireballs with the aid of lighter fluid. Adam tracked down the fire-eater's personal info and hired him for the party.

Once the party began, a few kids swam in the pool. Some kids hung out in the bouncy houses, while others watched the fire-eater perform his feats of fire consumption. He had set up right next to the mud-filled kiddie pools, which garnered little interest. The movies failed Adam once again. The fire-eater was a big hit. Everyone would shout out requests for how many fire-sticks the performer should swallow at a time.

The party was in full swing when Tanaka showed up with some friends. He was unassuming. Not really popular, but not exactly a kid who fell victim to any number of bullies who roamed the halls of Hilldale High.

As the night progressed many of the partygoers were inebriated. Tanaka spent most of his time by the pool drinking from a bottle of *Wild Turkey* he brought from home, swiping it from his father's liquor cabinet.

The bouncy houses were situated close together, near the back end of the yard underneath several large oak trees. Adam, sufficiently drunk himself, climbed one of the oak trees that looked out over the bouncy house. He climbed the tree for no real reason, but once he noticed he was perched above the bouncy houses, it was too perfect of a jumping opportunity to pass up.

After shouting for everyone to come watch him, Adam inched out on the biggest limb, which overlooked the purple and yellow bouncy house below.

He shouted, "Hilldale High School rules!" He jumped. He hit the inflatable floor and instantly shot back up in the air. He sailed into the adjacent bouncy house for a nice soft landing. It was unplanned, but perfect.

Once everyone saw that, they all wanted a turn. Teenager after teenager climbed the tree, shouted something new and jumped to the inflatable floor below in hopes of making it to the other bouncy house. All had succeeded in not injuring themselves, until Tanaka climbed the tree.

Tanaka was hammered. He struggled to get up on the limb, but once up there, he shouted something incoherent in Japanese and the only thing people understood was: "Tanaka-Bomb."

Everyone cheered.

Tanaka jumped, but he slipped on the limb, so he didn't land where he meant to on the first inflatable house. He bounced up and away from the second bouncy house. As he sailed in the air, the crowd cheered louder. He headed straight for the fire-eater

He landed on his butt with a thud. Mud splashed and hit the fire-eater and the kids gathered round enjoying the performance, now ruined. The mud in the fire-eater's face caused him to drop one of his fire-sticks. It fell into the mud where Tanaka sat, still smarting over his sore rear end.

Normally, this wouldn't be an issue. But the fire-eater had been performing his tricks for most of the night. Every time he doused the fire-sticks with lighter fluid there would be spillage on the ground below and what was at the feet of the fire-eater were two mud filled kiddie pools. Puddles of lighter fluid had formed in the kiddie pools, including in the one that Tanaka had just landed.

Once the lit fire-stick hit the puddle of lighter fluid, it took only seconds for the pool to ignite. Tanaka screamed a high-pitch scream that neighbors, who had called the police about the party, claimed to have heard the wail of a cat being tortured.

It wasn't a cat. It was Tanaka.

He crawled out of the pool. Pants on fire. He raced around the yard, looking for someone to help him. Everyone backed away. Most were laughing. Finally, Tanaka ran for the swimming pool. He jumped in the pool to put out the fire. As soon as Tanaka came up from the water, he noticed most of the party had gathered around the pool. Adam stood on the diving board. He pointed at Tanaka.

"Tanaka-Bomb!" Adam yelled.

The chant grew and grew, until the entire yard was saying the same thing, "Tanaka-Bomb! Tanaka-Bomb! Tanaka-Bomb!"

Tanaka did his best to hide his emotions. He tried to laugh it off, but when everyone noticed the fire had burned a whole through his pants to reveal his seared behind, Tanaka's smile faded. The entirety of the party roared with laughter as Tanaka ran from the pool and the party in embarrassment and shame.

* * *

Silence. Becky stared at the ground. Her mouth agape. She searched for something to say but found no words. Adam waited for her to respond, but Becky wouldn't make eye contact with him.

Adam said, "So, I mean, it's kind of a funny story."

Becky broke away from her blank stare. She glared at Adam. "Not for Jeff."

"No, I guess not," Adam agreed.

"Did people call him that after the party?" Becky asked.

He nodded. Profusely. He weighed in his head how many times he heard it throughout that school year. "Yeah, it had some legs, I guess. But it was high school. Everyone did stupid shit. Said things they regret. Did things we'd like to take back."

"We never had parties like that when I was in school," Becky said.

"That's one of your takeaways from that story?" Adam asked.

"No. You're also clearly an awful person."

"Awful?" Adam was shocked.

"Yeah. Awful," Becky said. "You're like the bad guy in all those high school movies."

"I didn't force Jeff to jump off that tree," Adam defended himself.

"Yeah, but you started the chant," she countered.

He quickly nodded. "This is true. But he gave himself that nickname. I just used it. I didn't think it would brand him for his life."

"You were involved in one of the most embarrassing times in his life. Every time he thinks of that night, I'm sure you're the face he sees. Pointing. Laughing at him. Calling him that name." Becky countered.

"I wasn't the only one doing those things."

"But you started it." Becky paused. "Do you think he's harboring some deep-seeded hatred for you. Wait. Who am I kidding? He definitely hates you."

"Hates me enough to aid and abet?" Adam worked the lead.

"Not everyone we meet that you wronged in high school wants to kill you." She thought about it. "They don't, right? How bad were you?"

"I was just like every other teenager who occasionally picked on people."

Becky eyed him. She studied his face, his eyes, to see if he wasn't being entirely honest with her.

"He was an asshole." Tanaka returned from the kitchen. He held a few plates of food with him. Eggs. Buttered rolls.

"Come on." Adam replied. "I wasn't worse than anyone else, was I?"

"Parker, you were a bully."

"You don't know that. We never really hung out in high school. Aside from that party, what was our only other interaction?"

"Not much."

"See." Adam pointed to Becky.

Tanaka continued, "Because I avoided you."

"Dammit," Adam cursed to himself.

"That night haunted me for some time. People from our class, to this day, still call me that nickname when we run into each other. But I made peace with it a long time ago. In fact, I don't even think about it much anymore." Tanaka grabbed a roll and took a bite.

"How'd you get over it?" Becky asked.

"Just time, I guess. I pretended like I didn't care. Ignored the comments and such. Eventually, it went away."

Adam waved his hand in the air. "Look. I can't change who I was. But that's not me now."

"You still tease Kevin," replied Becky.

"But we're friends. That's what friends do."

"You don't tease me," Becky said.

"Yeah, but that's different," Adam stuttered. "You're…"

"A girl?" She finished his sentence.

"That's not what I was going to say."

"Then finish it. What were you going to say?"

Adam opened his mouth. He said nothing. Looked to Tanaka, who was smiling. "You're on your own, Parker."

"Becky. We've got bigger things to worry about right now. Right?"

She crossed her arms over her chest. She agreed but didn't like Adam getting off the hook. "This conversation isn't over."

"Yeah, well. After we find Kevin, you can yell at me."

Tanaka asked, "Who's Kevin?"

"Our friend. He's in trouble," Becky answered.

"Kevin Simpson?"

"Yeah," Adam said.

"Really?" Tanaka was surprised. "He hangs out with you now?"

"Yeah. Why? We used to be friends before high school."

"Huh."

"What's that mean?" Adam was annoyed.

"Nothing. Just curious."

Adam sensed Tanaka holding back, but before he could press, Becky interjected. "Jeff. Do you know an Oliver Francis?"

Tanaka finished off the roll he grabbed before and looked to the ceiling, as if trying to pull a memory down from the faded, white paint. "Doesn't ring a bell." A voice from the kitchen called out. It was Tanaka's uncle again. He excused himself to check on the commotion.

Becky leaned in towards Adam, "Now what?"

"Why'd he'd act like me and Kevin couldn't be friends?"

"Focus! Kevin needs us," Becky snapped back. "We came here to learn about your awfulness. We did that. Where's the next clue?"

"You're right. Where would it be?" Adam remembered something else. "Awfulness? You know everyone isn't the best person they can possibly be when their teenagers."

"Well, I didn't terrorize a contingent of my peers during my youth strictly for me own enjoyment, so there's that."

"I hate you."

"We don't have time for that. Next clue."

Adam looked around the dining area. Nothing out of place. "Well, he would've left something here for us to find. Something out of place?"

"How do you leave something and ensure it remains for someone else to find?" Becky asked.

"You would hide it."

"What about the risk of someone finding it?"

"True. He could've snuck in last night and did it," Adam thought out loud.

"Or Jeff could be in on it," she offered.

"I thought of that, but I don't know. Doesn't seem like the insane-type."

"Clinical diagnosis?"

"Of course," Adam said. He continued. "How do you make sure something stays in a restaurant for someone else to find?"

Becky didn't answer. She got up from the table walked around the room. She looked at the paintings on the wall, the sculptures in their glass display cases, even under the tables. Adam remained seated. He didn't feel the need to pace the room searching for clues. He glanced from wall to wall, trying to spot something out of place.

"Found, found, found..." He repeated. A mantra to focus his thoughts. He stopped. Stood up. "Jeff!"

Tanaka came out of the kitchen.

"You have a lost and found?" Adam asked.

"Yeah." He pointed towards the front door.

Tanaka went to the podium typically used by the host and pulled a small cardboard box from the bottom shelf. He placed it on the table, in front of Adam. The marker on the side was faded, but legible. *L&F*

Adam dug his hands into the box. He pulled out a few kid's purses, some toys, a roller skate, scarves and hats. He placed everything on the table. Becky came over and sifted through the pile of lost items.

"Nothing. None of this stuff means anything to me," he said.

Becky held the roller skate in her hand. She flipped it around in her hand, examining the whole of it. She stopped. "Not all of it."

Adam grabbed the skate. Written in marker on the bottom of the metal frame read: *O. Francis.* Adam said, "Skateworld."

"That place closed years ago," Tanaka said. "Same time as Hilldale Video, where we're actually standing right now. This used to be the video store."

"Ha!" Adam shouted. He jammed his finger in Becky's face. "I told you! Hilldale Video."

"Whatever," she waved him off.

"Is that what you needed?" Tanaka asked.

"I think so. Yeah," Adam said, "Look, Jeff. I'm really sorry for what happened back then."

"You say that now, Parker. But I get the sense you haven't given it one thought until you found out who I was today. It's cool that you apologized, but it doesn't make me feel better about what you did."

Tanaka returned to the kitchen. Adam motioned to say more, but again, was at a loss for words.

"C'mon, Adam. We've got keep going." Becky said.

Adam nodded. He watched the swinging door of the kitchen close and Tanaka disappear from his sight. Adam was used to being disliked during the course of their investigations, but this was pure hatred. He couldn't shake that discomfort of knowing someone truly despised him.

# Chapter 15
# Kidnapped

The urge to vomit was strong with Kevin, but he held it down. It was quite the feat since he was known throughout the Simpson family as "The Squeamish One." Kevin wasn't a fan of the sight of blood. A scratch on the hand was no big deal, but if there was enough blood to create a drip then Kevin's gag reflex would engage. The moniker of "The Squeamish One" was given to him by his father who, the geek that he was, always liked to create handles for the people he loved. Although, Kevin never felt that love when everyone would laugh as he rushed to the bathroom when someone sliced their finger while cutting potatoes.

But not tonight. Maybe working alongside Adam for the last few months had desensitized Kevin to the gross nature of their business. He bent over, using his hand on the hood of the police car to keep him from falling. He hard-swallowed several times, choking back the urge to hurl, all while trying to forget the image from inside the police car.

Flashes came to him as he closed his eyes. Two officers. Dead. Throats slashed. Blood caked down their shirts, no longer pumping from the wound as they had died a long time ago.

Kevin stood up from his prone position, this time keeping his back turned to the police car. He didn't want to test his new-found resiliency. He took a deep breath, bringing in the cool night air. He took another. And another. With each inhale of oxygen, he regained his composure. But that quickly faded when thoughts turned to Adam. Two dead cops outside the house, meant that Adam was in trouble. Or worse. He ran to the house.

He raised his hand to knock on the front door but thought better of it. There could be someone inside with Adam, he thought. Kevin didn't want to alert them that he was at the front door. He stood there, hand raised as if ready to knock. He ran through scenarios of what was happening inside the house. Adam being beaten up. Tortured. Slapped around. Water-boarded. Kevin didn't know what waterboarding was exactly, but the way Nancy described it to him, he knew it wasn't good. More importantly, Kevin was still standing at the door. He needed to act.

He raced to the back of the house. No lights were on, so it was easy to go undetected. As he ran down the driveway, he looked to Becky's house. It was pitch black. Everyone was asleep. He thought about alerting her, but he didn't have time to stop. If Adam was in trouble, Kevin needed to act now. He climbed the back stairs with two monster steps.

He stopped. The back door was already opened.

Hairs on the back of his neck sprung to attention. He rubbed the tingly sensation from his neck with his hand. He entered the house, being careful not to make any noise. The door creaked as he pushed it further open. Kevin cringed. He already failed at a quiet entry. He waited. No movement. No sounds. Maybe he was alone, Kevin thought.

He walked into the kitchen. He stopped. He listened for signs of life. Breathing. Feet moving on the carpet. Anything to clue Kevin as to what was happening. He was a statue in the middle of the kitchen. He ran through another list of potential situations involving Adam.

He could be hanging upside down in the basement as a team of men worked his body over with baseball bats. Maybe he was in the middle of a circle of guys and they each took turns smacking Adam around. He could have electrodes attached to his groin. That last one was too much of a reminder from their dealings with the Scout. Kevin tried to forget that fateful night in the shed four months ago. Ultimately, Kevin decided to check one room at a time. As soon as he turned for the dining room, the kitchen lights clicked on.

Stunned. He stood up straight, "What the…"

And then blackness.

He awoke in the dark. His head pounding. The knot on the back of his head throbbed. He called out, but there was tape around his mouth. He tried to move, but he was also taped to the chair. He looked to his groin. No electrodes. He breathed easy.

Voices from the other room. Muffled at times, but he thought he heard Adam. He screamed from under the tape gag, but it was pointless. He rocked in his chair. The closet was too tight of a fit, so he made very little work of improving his position. The voices grew closer.

The door handle moved. Then a rush of light. The door was opened. Adam stared at him. He was also tied to a chair. He yelled. Kevin couldn't make out who he was talking to, as the man's back was to him. Kevin screamed, but again, nothing. A gun was placed to his head. Kevin froze. He looked to Adam, who pleaded with the man holding the gun. The gun barrel was pushed harder into his head. Kevin winced. Adam promised he would save him, but Kevin wasn't too sure from what or who. The gun was removed. The man walked over to Adam. He blocked Kevin's view. His hand raised, butt of the gun firm in its grip. He brought his hand down. When he moved aside, Adam remained still in the chair. He was unconscious.

The man turned to face Kevin. He smiled. He was small in stature. His hair was down to his shoulders. Stringy. Black. "Hang tight, Kevin. We'll talk soon." He shut the door. Back in darkness.

Kevin heard movement on the other side of the door. Sounded like Adam was being picked up or dragged. The front door closed shut and the last thing Kevin heard was the sound of a car driving away. He fought to free himself, but nothing he did worked. He was trapped in the closet.

Hours later, the front door slammed shut again. This woke Kevin from his slumber. He had dozed off in the chair. He listened again. More movement and then, the closet door opened. The same man. He smiled. He got behind the chair, leaned it back and pushed it forward out of the closet. The man struggled pushing the chair. Kevin heard him grunt and gasp with each push. He suddenly became self-conscious of his big frame, but then the chair moved. The trip out of the closet was still tough for the stringy-haired man. Kevin wondered how the man even got him in the chair in the first place.

It was a cabin. Kevin was placed in the living room. The furniture looked like someone chopped a few trees down and bought cushions. The man took a seat on the couch.

"Now, I'm going to remove the gag, so we can talk. Please don't scream. No one can hear you. We are far away from everyone. All I want to do is talk. Ok?"

Kevin nodded. He wanted that thing out of his mouth. The man ripped the tape from Kevin's mouth. Kevin spit out a wad of rolled-up cloth and screamed. His mouth and face on fire from the tape removal.

"I thought we agreed on not screaming," the man said.

"The tape! It stings." Kevin flexed his mouth to ease the pain.

"Sorry. I should've warned you."

"Where's Adam?"

"I don't want to talk about Parker."

"But I do."

The man sighed. "Thirsty?" He was up and in the kitchen.

The faucet turned on. Kevin heard the sound of water filling a glass. He couldn't turn around because of the tape wrapped around his hands, legs and the chair. "Did you kill him?" Kevin asked.

A laugh. The man returned with the glass of water and a knife. "Not yet." He sliced the tape on one of Kevin's wrists, freeing the hand. Kevin took the glass of water. He drank most of it while the man watched.

"Are you going to torture me?"

"I hadn't planned on it."

"Kill me?"

"You're not the reason why I'm in Hilldale."

"This is about Adam."

"Isn't it always?"

Kevin had no response. He agreed with his captor. "Who are you?" He took another big swig from the glass.

"Oliver Francis."

"Who?"

"We went to school together. I was a freshman when you were a senior. I don't think we knew each other back then, although our paths did cross at times."

"How so?" He held up his empty glass. "Can I have some more?"

Francis smiled. Progress was being made. He grabbed the glass and headed to the kitchen, continuing the conversation. "Our story isn't that dissimilar. Smart. Honor roll every semester. A bit of a nerd for things. Not a lot of girls interested in us, And of course, the bullying."

"I've been told it's a part of growing up."

The faucet continued to run. "So is the situation we're in. Growing up."

"What situation is that?"

"The world of Adam Parker crashing down all around him." The faucet shut off. Francis returned with another full glass of water. He took a seat opposite Kevin. "Let me tell you my story."

Francis gave a brief overview of what his high school was like. The consistent mocking at the hands of Adam and Fred every morning and the state of unease it put him in throughout the school year.

"Every morning. Really?" Kevin asked.

"Like clockwork."

"Why didn't you complain to a teacher? Get your locker moved?"

"I was fourteen years-old. What did I know back then?" Francis was up now. He paced the living room. "Sure. Looking back, I'm sure I could've done a lot of things different. But the man you see in front of you now was not the same when he was fourteen. Were you?"

"Fair point."

"Exactly. Being a teenager is like living in the forest. You have no idea that on the other side is a meadow. All you see is trees. Darkness. Constant fear."

"We had different experiences growing up."

Francis smiled upon hearing Kevin's reluctance to believe. He returned to the couch. "You tell yourself that. But you and I both know, that's a lie."

"Believe what you want."

"I looked you up, Kevin Simpson. It was only fair since I've been planning this whole thing for quite some time. You're Adam's best friend. I had to learn about you."

"That's right. I am his best friend. And he'll stop at nothing to rescue me." Kevin was defiant.

"But you weren't always his best friend."

Kevin hesitated. "Well, he moved away."

"You know I'm talking about high school. He dropped you when he realized popularity was within his grasp."

"You make it sound like it's some kind of competition."

"It is!" Francis shot up from his seat. "All of it is. Don't you see? Adam was funny. Good looking. He had a leg up on everyone. People liked him. He didn't have to try to gain affection. He simply got it."

"Leg up for what?"

"To be cool. To be popular. To walk the hallways and get high-fives and smiles. Did you ever walk the halls of school and get that? Or did you slink along the wall, hoping no one would see you. Praying that no one would realize that they hadn't made fun of you in a while." Francis was emotional, his rage mounting. "Did you wait inside the classroom until the hall was almost empty before you headed to your next class? Being late to class was an easier pill to swallow than having half the school laugh at you. No one calling you by your name. Everyone using the nickname that some idiot senior gave you during the first week of freshman year. Same Pants. Same Pants. SAME PANTS!"

Francis flipped over the coffee table, spilling its contents on the floor of the cabin. He spun around. Stared out the window. His back to Kevin, who remained still. Francis's chest heaved with each deep breath, bringing his boiling rage down to a simmer. "When this is done, you'll feel this anger, too. You're going to learn a few things about your best friend."

# Chapter 16
## Progress?

Kenney stood in the middle of his office. His desk littered with papers and file folders, none of which were in any order. He stared out the window that overlooked the side-lot. Nothing but civilian cars and the occasional stray dog, which made Kenney wonder if Hilldale had a feral dog problem.

There was a knock on the office door as it opened. He turned to find Officer Pete Donaldson. Donaldson joined the force five months ago. As most rookies were, he was eager and inexperienced. Smart, but not always common-sense smart. Tall, lanky and hardly a bit of stubble on his face. Not because he always shaved, but because he rarely had reason.

"Chief. You asked for me?" Donaldson stood by the door, his hand still on the handle. Half in the office, half out.

Kenney sat behind his desk. "How'd the door to door go this morning?"

"Not bad," He pulled a notebook from his back pocket and flipped through it as he stepped into the office. Donaldson worked the scene in front Parker's house this morning. "Most neighbors didn't see anything. A few heard a car, but not sure when or even if it was on their street. Had a couple complaints about the cop car being on the street."

"Christ, Donaldson," Kenney complained, "You said this was 'not bad'. This is nothing."

"I know. Sorry, Chief. But that got me thinking. Maybe the action wasn't on the street. Maybe they came from one of the other streets. Like through the back yards. So, I went door-to-door on the neighboring streets."

"Wait. Did you just get back?"

Donaldson hesitated. "Uh, yeah. Sorry, was I supposed to be here for something?"

"No. I just thought you were already here. I mean, I called for you a few times. No wonder you didn't...forget it. What did you find out?"

He flipped some more through the notebook. "I spoke with woman who said she heard a car earlier in the night and then again later."

"What was it doing?"

"Parked. Then started up and drove away."

"That could be someone being picked up. That's not helpful."

Donaldson flipped the page. "I then spoke with an elderly man who says he saw two people exit out of his neighbor's back yard. Enter a car and drive away. He thought it was odd, since his neighbor is away on vacation."

"What time did this happen?"

"Early evening."

Kenney placed his hands on the back of his head. He interlocked his fingers and stretched as he processed the information. "Ok. That could be Parker and his accomplice leaving for Brookville."

"Why'd they go to Brookville?"

"Because Parker is a pain in the ass. Anything else?"

He flipped the notebook shut. "Nothing of note."

"All right," Kenney was up. He grabbed his jacket from the coat rack behind him. "Go back to the old man's house. Find out if he heard a second car later in the night."

"Wait. A second car?" Donaldson was confused.

"Parker was taken from his house. And if no one on his street saw anything, I'm betting he was escorted out the back door. Same escape route he used for his Brookville trip."

"And the old man knows this?"

"I wouldn't be surprised if this man knows everything about his street. Keep digging."

"Where are you going, Chief?" Donaldson asked.

"Brookville."

\* \* \*

Adam and Becky stood in front of Nancy's front door. They were there for a while, not really sure how to proceed with the conversation they needed to have but were dreading. Nancy was intense and if Becky's assumptions were accurate, she was deeply invested in Kevin. Finding out he's been kidnapped may put a charge in her that they might not survive.

"Knock," Adam started.

"You knock. He's your best friend." Becky countered.

"Yeah, but you could soften the blow because you're a woman."

Becky punched him in the arm. Hard. He winced. "I'll do it." He skulked up the steps. Before he could knock, the door whipped open. Nancy stood in the doorway. Smirk on her face.

"About time. I've been watching you two for about ten minutes."

"How?" Becky asked.

Nancy pointed to the camera above the door.

"How paranoid *are* you?" Adam asked.

"It's not paranoia. It's being prepared. What's going on?"

"Uh...Becky has something she'd like to..." Another punch from Becky to the exact same spot on his arm. "C'mon!" He rubbed his soon-to-be black and blue arm.

Nancy sensed something was wrong. "Where's Kevin? I've been texting him all morning, but he's not texting back."

Adam sighed. "There's been a development in the case."

Nancy got in Adam's face. "Tell me right now, Parker. What's going on?"

"Kevin has been kidnapped," he blurted out. "I was taken the other night to this cabin where some psycho from my past blames me for his shitty life and he's holding Kevin as collateral."

"Collateral for what?"

"To make sure I go through with this ridiculous game."

"Game? What kind of game?"

"Some sort of trip-down-memory-lane kind of game."

Nancy opened her mouth to speak, but she couldn't hone in on a question. She had many. They all circled around Kevin. It was too much to process. Her emotions were high. She had to slow it down. She sat on her front step. Took a deep breath. "Please. Explain it to me. From the beginning."

Her eyes grew hazy. She placed her face in her hands. Hiding her tears. Becky sat next to her, arm around her shoulder. Adam knelt in front of her. He relayed the story of his night and their trip to *The Slammin' Sushi*.

As Adam finished his story, Nancy wiped her face dry. She stood up. "I remember Tanaka. He was a nice guy, but he hated you."

"We got that impression," Becky said.

Nancy looked to Adam, "Like, you couldn't say your name around him or he'd go into some rant about wanting to make you pay."

"He seemed to calm down when we talked to him."

"This was back in school, so maybe he forgave you."

Adam winced. "Not completely."

"And you're sure Kevin is okay?" Nancy asked.

"As long as we play this game. Yes. I think he'll be fine." Adam paused. "This is about me. Not him."

"What happens when you finish?"

"Kevin is set free and I'm probably killed," he deadpanned. Adam was scared, but he really didn't have a frame of reference for what Francis's plans were, so he couldn't contemplate his demise or have time to get upset over it.

Becky interrupted. "Which is what we're trying to avoid, Nancy. We thought it would be best to tell you about Kevin."

Nancy nodded. She stood up. Said nothing and went back into her house. The door shut behind her, leaving Adam and Becky alone. Adam opened his mouth to speak, but the front door swung back open. Nancy returned, backpack slung over her shoulder.

"Who's driving?"

Adam started, "Wait. You don't have…"

"My boyfriend is being held captive by someone you created. I'm not staying home, waiting for you to do something. Who's driving?"

Becky raised her hand. She followed Nancy to the car.

Adam whispered to himself, "Boyfriend. I knew it."

# Chapter 17
## Kevin's Lament

Kevin was tied to the chair for most of the morning, but Francis moved him closer to the window, so he could look out over the forest below. From what he could see, the cabin was situated atop of a hill that overlooked some part of the Hilldale if they were even in Hilldale. There were not many forests in town, except on the end that bordered Wellsboro. He thought he might ask Francis, but he knew he couldn't trust anything he said.

He got the impression that Francis was trying to be his friend. To make him understand his plight, his reason why Kevin was tied to a chair. Kevin sort-of understood. He knew the pain Francis spoke of. He felt a lot of those same emotions during his own high school days. Ostracized by others for being who you were. Kids laughing at you simply because others were doing it. No one coming to your aid. Not one person helping, out of fear of receiving the same ridicule.

Kevin didn't doubt Francis's anger towards Adam. Kevin just never was witness to it back in high school. Adam and Kevin never really crossed paths in high school. Sometimes, there'd be a shared nod between old friends. Maybe even a few words of catching up, but nothing ever in depth. Kevin had his friends. Adam had his friends. And never did they interact with each other.

Francis returned from the outside. He repeatedly escaped to the front of the cabin, like a smoker, but Kevin never noticed any packs of cigarettes. Plus, his clothes never smelled of stale smoke. This last time, Kevin thought he heard a car engine, but didn't hear anything else so he left it alone.

Francis plopped down on the couch, next to Kevin. They both faced the trees below. "Pretty, right?"

"Yeah. I can't really place it."

"I'm not going to tell you where we are, so don't go fishing." He slapped Kevin on the shoulder encouraged by his attempt.

"I guess I had to try."

"I don't blame you."

They took in the view for a few more seconds in silence. Francis took a deep breath and let it out. "So, who was it for you? Your freshman year."

"What do you mean?" Kevin asked.

"You know what I mean. Who terrorized you when you first went to Hilldale High?"

Kevin paused. "I had a pretty normal high school experience. Much like anyone else growing up in Hilldale."

"Kevin." Francis leaned forward, to get into Kevin's peripheral. Kevin turned to face him. "Don't lie. I told you. I already know most of these things."

"Then why ask?"

Francis shot back in his seat. Leaned against the cushions of the couch. "Because. I'm trying to create a dialogue with you."

"For what purpose?"

"C'mon. Who was it?"

Kevin sighed. He was lying before, but not out of some twisted notion of fear to name names, but because he didn't want to connect with Francis on any level.

"Stop overthinking this." Francis sensed the reason for his trepidation. "We're just talking."

"Can you blame me? I'm tied up. You've shoved a gun to my head and threatened to kill me if Adam doesn't do what you say."

"Or if you don't answer my questions."

He froze. Kevin forgot about that incentive. He heard a chuckle from Francis on the couch. Check-mate.

"It was one kid, all right?  Some kids from the football team. George Waters. Jacob Lansing. Couple others."

"There you go. Now we're sharing." Another encouraging slap on the shoulder. "What'd they do?"

"C'mon, I told you. I don't really want to relive this, okay?"

Francis's hands went up. "I get it. It's easier to forget about it. To pretend it didn't happen, so it doesn't haunt you for all your days. But then you become victim to it, without even knowing it. You ignore one of the most influential moments of your existence and all that does is shape you as a person for the rest of your life."

"It was *just* high school."

"Were you always shy? Did you always keep to yourself, never trying to make new friends?"

"I have friends."

"Parker and the Wilson girl. That's it. Am I right?"

"It's Clarkson now. She got married. And I have other friends. People I work with at the movie theater. We're friends."

"You left that job two months ago."

"How do you know that?"

"I didn't come up with this plan overnight, Kevin. I told you already. I planned this. I researched Adam. Becky. You." Francis stood up. He walked in front of the window, blocking Kevin's view. "These friends at the theater. You see any of them after you left?"

"I guess not," Kevin admitted.

"So, they're not your friends. No. You have two friends. Adam and Becky."

Kevin nodded.

"See! You're lying again!"

"What? I just nodded."

"What about Nancy Olliver?"

Kevin stopped. He didn't forget about Nancy, he just didn't want to bring her up. He didn't want Francis knowing about her. He didn't want her dragged into this. "What about her?"

"She's your girlfriend. Notice, I'm not asking you."

"She has nothing to do with this."

"Not yet, she doesn't. But I suspect she'll find out about you being my hostage and force herself onto the team, as you guys claim to be."

"Leave her alone!"

"That depends."

"On what?"

"On your willingness to quit jerking me around and tell me about," Francis produced air-quotes, "...some kids on the football team. Tell me about tryouts."

Kevin's face contorted. He looked to the floor. Instantly, his cheeks went red. Embarrassment mixed with anger and rage. He worked extremely hard to put that incident in his past. Chalked it up to the experience of high school. Part of growing up. Can't take everything so seriously. As soon as Francis mentioned it, all of those comforting phrases crumbled and left feelings of sadness, regret and anger. So much anger.

Francis smiled as Kevin raised his head from the floor. He met his captor's face with a glare.

Francis was excited. It was story time.

*　*　*

Kevin never minded his weight too much. In fact, it was never an issue while growing up through elementary school. His parents were not into sports, unless it was a reference to a *Star Trek* episode and even then, they just liked to talk about it. They never actually did anything in a physical sense. This meant there was no pressure from his parents to "be active" or play sports when he was younger.

Most kids have parents who sign them up for everything. A different sport for a different season. Soccer in the fall, basketball in the winter, baseball in the spring and come summertime, you were forced outside to play in the sun. Kevin never had that pressure. He watched movies and wrote stories. He played video games. And he liked to eat.

When he began middle school, kids teased him about his size. They'd make fat jokes and Kevin would laugh them off. But the jokes didn't stop. It bothered him, like it would anyone who was subjected to the consistent taunting of middle school kids.

When high school started, the teasing didn't stop, and it got meaner. Not only verbal, but physical. Kevin was knocked down often when he walked the halls. He was laughed at in the cafeteria as he ate lunch. The main offender was Carson Owens. He picked on Kevin almost every day of freshman year.

Owens was a junior when Kevin entered Hilldale High. He was also the starting quarterback for the football team, so he was admired by many of the kids in school and even a few faculty members, who usually did nothing to stop the teasing. Not because they didn't care, but they never witnessed it nor believed it to be true. *"Not Carson. He was such a nice guy."*

Owens walked the hallway between classes with a gaggle of teenagers in tow. Back then, Kevin thought it similar to one of the many dramas about high school life that saturated 90s television. Owens and his gang looking to cause trouble, while the hero of the tale, Kevin, would struggle to be the best version of himself. And maybe teach a lesson along the way. But this wasn't a melodrama pulled from the *CW*. This was reality. And reality sucked.

Kevin looked to avoid the pack of Owens followers, but he wasn't always successful. If Owens saw him, he'd shout out something like "Pork Chop Express!" or "Baa Ram Ewe!" Not only was Owens a bully but he would use movie references to do it, which really annoyed Kevin. It was a slap to the face. Kevin liked most of the movies Owens referenced, which he also stopped watching because inevitably he equated those films with being bullied.

Sophomore year, Kevin got proactive. Coach Douglas asked him if he'd be interested in trying out for the football team on account of his large frame. *"We need an O-lineman"* was what Coach Douglas told Kevin a few times throughout the last month of freshman year. Kevin had no idea what that meant. But it stuck with him when he saw the tryout notice in the school paper. It wasn't something he wanted to do, but rather thought he had to do in order to stop the Owens abuse.

If he was part of the football team, maybe Owens would back off. It was a hair-brained idea, but it was the only idea Kevin thought would work. Other than leaving town, but that wasn't an option. At least, that's what his father told him when Kevin begged them to move.

That August before his sophomore year, he spent a week trying out for the football team. He didn't really mind it, too much. Just sticking his body in front of people. He didn't know if he was doing a good job or not. All the coaches, including Coach Douglas, would yell constantly about a variety of things. None of it made any sense. Kevin thought he should learn the vernacular but decided if this experiment worked and he made the team, he would do it then. Seemed like a waste of his time to learn it now.

One the third day of tryouts, Owens showed up to check out the potential new recruits. It didn't take long before he spotted Kevin running drills along the sideline.

"Ice box!" Owens yelled out from across the field.

Kevin cursed to himself. Another movie reference.

"You're trying out!?" Owens shouted again. The group of friends around him started laughing and pointing.

Kevin didn't want to have conversation across the field, over dozens of people. Thankfully, Coach Douglas told Owens to *"Shut it"*. The try-outs returned to normal, but Kevin spied Owens continuing to laugh and joke with his posse.

At the end of the day, Kevin hit the showers. Many of the kids already showered and left for the day. Kevin wasn't a big fan of the group shower. While he eased up on his anxiety of having the other teenage boys see him naked, he preferred to wait until the showers were not as crowded. So, usually he washed up with a few other potential members of the team, but on this day, he was showering alone.

He wrapped an over-used, over-washed school towel around his waist and headed for the locker room. As he turned the corner, he found Owens waiting for him. He leaned against a locker, smile across his face.

"How were tryouts?"

"Okay, I guess." Kevin was nervous.

"You think you got a shot?" He pushed off from the locker and walked closer to Kevin.

"Maybe. I don't know."

"I never pegged you for the sports type, Chunk."

"Yeah, well. People change, right?"

Owens laughed. "Nah. People don't change. Some try, sure. But they either fail, give up or need to be told the reality of the situation." He was no longer smiling.

"Are you being serious?" Kevin asked.

"I don't like you, Simpson." The use of his real name threw Kevin into a panic. "You're a loser. It's just how it is. And losers don't play football. Not with me."

Kevin tried to salvage the conversation. "C'mon, Carson. What if I can help the team?"

Another laugh. "Have you seen yourself out there? You look like a manatee trying to walk. We laughed at you the whole tryout."

"What's your problem with me? I didn't do anything to you."

"I don't need to have a problem with you. I just like making fun of you. Everyone has a good time at your expense. It makes the school year go by faster, that's all."

"That's stupid," Kevin shot back.

"So is leaving your locker unlocked while in the shower."

Kevin spun around to see his clothes missing. The entire locker empty. Owens wrenched the towel from his waist. Kevin reached out to grab it, but Owens was ready for him. He shoved Kevin to the ground. His naked backside smacked on the concrete floor of the locker room. He was sprawled out, completely naked in front of Owens who was laughing.

"Look at that little dick. Ha! Little, baby dick!" Owens pointed and laughed.

The locker room doors opened, and Owens crew came in. Boys and girls, as if waiting for their cue, entered the room to find Kevin on the floor. Naked.

More laughter. More name calling.

Kevin scrambled to find something to hide behind. He ran into the stacks of lockers, but Owens and friends followed him. Laughing at every move he made. A wall prevented his escape. Lockers on either side of him. He was trapped. He found a helmet and placed it over his genitals. This only spurred the laughter on more. Owens laughed so hard, he fell to the ground.

Kevin stood there listening to everyone laughing. Watching them point. He looked to the ground, so as not to make eye contact. He didn't want them to see the tears that rolled down his cheeks.

Then there was shouting. Coach Douglas heard the commotion and came upon all of them in the locker room.

He shouted for everyone to get out. Instantly, the crew split up and left the locker room. He found Owens on the floor, still laughing.

"Owens! Get up."

Owens took his time. "Sorry, coach. Just having some fun."

Douglas looked to Kevin. He smirked. He lightly slapped Owens on the back of the head. "Get out of here. See you, Monday."

Owens gave one last look to Kevin. Laughed himself out the locker room, leaving Coach Douglas and Kevin alone.

"Where are your clothes, Simpson?"

"Don't know. I think they took them."

Douglas sighed. "All right. I'll grab you some sweats."

"Coach." Kevin said. Douglas paused and looked to him. "Did I make the team?"

Another sigh. "Sorry, kid. It ain't your day, apparently." Douglas left to find sweats for Kevin, who choked back more tears.

* * *

Kevin wiped his face clear of emotion, hoping Francis didn't see the tears from having to relive the story. He wasn't concerned about giving Francis the upper hand. He never wanted others to know what had happened to him that day. He never forgot about it. He just ignored it. Pretended it didn't happen.

Francis had his back to Kevin. He was looking out the window to allow the emotion in the room to settle. "And you never told anyone that story before?"

"No. Never. It's no one's business." Kevin sat upright in the chair. He cleared his throat, choking down the sadness.

"Yes. That's true. But that's not why you kept it to yourself."

"Sure. I was embarrassed. I'm still to this day. Wouldn't you be?"

Francis smiled. He turned around. "I was embarrassed for all my years in high school. Those four years were my personal hell. Me and you. We're alike."

"I'm not murdering people."

"Give it time. If you let go of your shame; if you realized the power you hand over to others. The unsaid permission to abuse you, make jokes at your behalf, treat you like a sidekick. "

"Adam is my friend. I told you. He's changed. He's not the same kid he was in high school. None of us are."

"Even Carson Owens?"

Kevin paused. "Even him."

"He continued to torment you that year, didn't he?"

"Yeah. And the year after that. He never let me forget that day. And they told others, I know. I'm sure you heard it from someone who heard it from someone. Like some urban legend. Even my senior year, some asshole would bring it up. People would laugh, and I'd laugh with them, so they didn't think it bothered me."

"I understand that survival instinct to fit in. Laugh at the jokes with them to lessen the pain. Yes, I know it too well," Francis switched gears. "But don't you see? You're doing that, now. With Adam. You play along with his jokes, don't you?"

Kevin shook his head. "No, we're friends. Friends tease each other."

"We don't change after high school, Kevin. We simply evolve into better or worse versions of our adolescence selves. Parker is a bully. He will always be a bully, but now he's wrapped it up with charm and comradery."

"You're wrong. You're just wrong about all of it."

"I told you we were alike. Not because we hold the bond of being victims, but because our tormenter is one in the same. Adam Parker is just as much a bully to you as he was to me all those years ago. The difference is you're in denial about it."

"And making Adam go through this ridiculous challenge is going to solve that?" Kevin shot back.

"No. It's going to remind him of how bad of a person he truly is and then I'm going to bring his world crashing down."

"How?"

Francis smiled. Kevin waited for the answer, but it wasn't coming. The smile never faded on Francis's face as he patted Kevin's shoulder on his wat to the kitchen. "You'll see."

# Chapter 18
## Follow the Club

Kenney made it a point to avoid Brookville. The town had its own sordid history that caused anyone who ventured within its borders to immediately grow uneasy. While most people who lived outside of Brookville were scared to talk about the eerie happenings that occurred within the town; the townsfolk accepted it as their reality, even relished in the uniqueness of Brookville's story. Kenney's reasons for avoiding the town were less supernatural in nature. It was a woman.

Kenney didn't like to date. He hated everything about courting a woman. He turned to online dating sites to find a match, as these sites like to proclaim they can do. One of the sites matched him up with a shopkeeper in Brookville. They dated for a few months and everything was going well. Kenney enjoyed her company until the shopkeeper started talking about marriage and kids, wanting to know if Kenney would move to Brookville or "force her to move to that crummy town of Hilldale."

Immediately, Kenney took a step back from the relationship. That resulted in a very public display of rage on the shopkeeper's part while they were enjoying a meal at one of Brookville's eateries. The commotion brought about an official introduction between Kenney and Sheriff Copeland as the police were called to the restaurant to deal with a 'possible domestic incident.'

Sheriff Copeland knew the shopkeeper from back in school and he wasn't surprised by her reaction to being dumped. He assuaged his classmate's hurt feelings and extradited Kenney from the situation with ease. There was a mutual understanding between the two men after that. Kenney prided himself on his relationships with fellow officers from other towns, especially Copeland. The foundation of a good working relationship between towns started with respect between the police departments.

"Get out of my town." Copeland stood behind his desk. Arms folded.

Kenney paused mid-sit. He stood up. "What's that?"

"You heard me. Get out. I don't want anything to do with whatever it is you've got cooking in Hilldale."

"I don't know want we've got *cooking*, to be honest."

"Word has it, you've got a madman on the loose in your town. The same two kids I ran out of town for crashing a funeral were kidnapped."

Kenney cleared his throat. "Not sure how you know any of that."

"Gossip crosses departments. You know that, Chief. Dispatchers talk. EMTs talk. Officers talk. Shit. I bet someone posted it on Facebook."

"Anyway," Kenney attempted to change the subject. "I'm not planning on staying long. I just wanted to ask about a case. The murder at the golf course."

"Didn't I just say I don't want to be involved?"

"Yes. And I'm ignoring that. You know, because you're a cop. And this is what cops do. They compare notes and help other cops. I don't pretend to know what goes on in your town, but I need to find this guy who's causing trouble in mine."

Copeland paused. He looked around the room, as if waiting for a sign. He looked to his computer. He leaned forward in his chair and tapped at the keyboard. He positioned his face in front of the webcam. Red lights flashed around his eyes. The computer unlocked.

"Retinal scan?" Kenney asked.

"We had some security concerns the other night. Seems we were asked to upgrade some things."

"Asked? By who?"

Copeland stared straight ahead. Kenney already knew the answer. He nodded. Copeland returned his attention to the computer screen. He dragged the mouse; double-clicked to open a file. "What do you want to know about the Thompson murder?"

"Did anything jump out?"

"Stabbed multiple times with a golf club. A 3-iron. The head came off and the shaft was filed down to a point."

"That takes a while, no?" Kenney asked.

"I assume so."

"But why the golf course?"

"We think it was opportunity. Stalked him a bit. Got his routine down and chose the golf course for the kill. Blended in with the golfers and waited for his chance."

"You think the perp is a guy?" Kenney asked. He leaned forward in his seat.

"I know *you* do."

"Oliver Francis."

Copeland tapped the keyboard again. "I got nothing."

"Crime scene photos?"

He swung the computer monitor around to show Kenney. Photos littered the screen. Kenney stood up and got closer to the monitor. He examined the different pictures. They were in rows and columns. Smaller, but discernable.

He pointed to one of the pictures. "Can you blow that one up?"

The screen filled with one picture. Bottom of the tree. Thompson's back visible on the other side. Red smears on his shirt where blood had dried. The head of the 3-iron laid on the ground beside the tree. Kenney looked closer.

"Can you zoom in? On the club head."

"What do you see?" Copeland asked.

"Something's written on the bottom."

The screen changed to a blown-up image of just the club head. Copeland was up from his seat as well. He leaned forward on his desk. "Hang on. I can enhance that."

A few clicks later and the blurry image was made clearer. An inscription on the bottom of the club head read: *Property of B.S.*

"Do you know what that means?" Kenney asked him.

Copeland nodded, but he wasn't happy about knowing. "Brookville Sanitarium. Son of a bitch." He scraped his keys off his desk. "I'll drive."

* * *

Brookville Sanitarium sat atop a large hill which overlooked the town reservoir. The hill was littered with trees, rocks and most of the town's animal population. Reservoir land was usually protected land, which meant there was a large chain-link fence around the property to keep the people from venturing to close to the water supply. In the case of the land surrounding Brookville Sanitarium, there was another chain-link fence around the perimeter to keep the guests from venturing into town. This fence was taller and meaner looking with several strands of barb wire decorating the top as an added deterrent for the residents of the sanitarium.

Accompanying the Brookville Sanitarium was a detailed account of horror stories and strange tales. Much of it was exaggerated fiction or blatant lies, but there were some stories from behind the sanitarium walls that were very true and equally disturbing and one of the many secrets that Brookville's main benefactor, John Thornton, protected from the outside world.

Copeland didn't say much during the ride to the sanitarium. When he did speak it was mainly about the random stories that people gossiped about, but he talked like he was in mid-conversation which made it hard for Kenney to understand what he was actually talking about.

"Didn't happen like they said."

"Huh?" Kenney dozed off while looking out his window.

"The escape."

He shifted in his seat. Alert. "There was an escape?"

"Not now. Back in '54. Papers got it wrong."

Copeland mumbled about the newspapers again and focused on the road, leaving Kenney in a state of confusion.

"The reason they gave was only half-true," Copeland said.

"What reason? What are you talking about?" Kenney asked.

"The double-homicide on the third floor."

"Of the sanitarium?"

"Yeah. Back in '87."

"Sheriff, I have no idea what you're talking about." Kenney professed.

Copeland nodded. He drove the rest of the way in silence. Kenney's confusion was greater than his curiosity. The sooner he was out of this town, the better. The thought of hunting a madman in his own town was suddenly more calming than a simple drive through Brookville.

Copeland took the turn up the long winding round that circled the hill and led to the sanitarium. They arrived at the front gate to a guard holding out his hand for the car to stop. He hemmed and hawed about unsuspecting visitors and needing permission. It didn't matter that the Brookville's sheriff was glaring back at him.

Copeland was in no mood for the delay. He shouted about who he was and what his badge allowed him to do, all colored with a variety of obscenities until finally, the guard relented. Kenney noticed the guard's middle finger raised high as they drove up the remaining portion of the hill.

The driveway forked at the top, one way leading to a small parking lot for visitors and employees while the other road coiled around to the front entrance for easy pick-up and drop-off. Copeland took the second route and parked the cruiser at the front doors.

They were greeted by a small man. Glasses. Horned rimmed. Kenney expected a white-lab coat but settled for tan *Dockers* and a red polo shirt. The man smiled. This was Dabney Wendell; head of the Brookville Sanitarium.

"Dabney. Sorry for the intrusion," Copeland said. He wasn't apologetic, but rather matter-of-fact.

"Sheriff. It's always nice to see you."

"Dabney, this is Chief Kenney of the Hilldale Police Department."

Kenney held his hand up. A frozen wave. Wendell approached and shook his hand. "Pleasure. What brings you to these parts?"

Copeland didn't give him a chance to reply. "It's actually my case. His case is related."

"The murder? The Thompson fella?" Wendell asked.

"Yup." Copeland stepped closer to Wendell as if mindful of eavesdroppers, which Kenney found odd since the three of them were the only people out front. Nevertheless, Copeland spoke in hushed tones. "Murder weapon was from one of your golf bags. It belonged to the sanitarium."

Wendell paused. "You're sure?"

"How many guests do you have here at the sanitarium?" Kenney asked.

"Eighty-nine. There are several wings to the main house where most of the other guests reside. My office is on the second floor."

"Are most of the people here...troubled?" Kenney asked.

"Quite. That is why many of our guests come here. Some need a bit more help than others, no doubt. I admit, the term *sanitarium* does hold a negative connotation in some circles, but we are a healing facility and we are very successful. Of course, when guests first arrive, they are not at their best."

"Has anyone gone missing?" Kenney asked.

This hurt Wendell. "Chief Kenney, I take great pride in my work here. Certainly, enough pride to keep my guests on the premises."

"Relax, Dabney. It's a fair question," Copeland said.

"Sheriff, you would know as soon as I would if someone broke out of here," Wendell inferred.

Kenney picked up on it. "What does he mean?" He asked Copeland.

"The security system is tapped into the station. If any alarms go off, we go off." Copeland replied, then he placed his arm on Wendell's shoulder. "We have to look around. I'm sorry."

"No, you don't," Wendell replied.

Copeland smiled. "We do."

"No," he held Copeland's gaze. "You don't."

"Oliver Francis." Kenney said.

Wendell paused. He nodded.

"He was healed?"

"Oliver was a guest here for a long time. He knew all of the employees by first name and he was always a pleasure. It only made sense that his recovery was complete."

"When was he released?" Copeland's turn to ask questions.

"About three months ago. It took us by surprise, actually."

"How exactly?" Kenney asked.

"When Oliver arrived, he was depressed. Distraught over his life or, rather, what it had become."

"What was wrong with him?"

Wendell smiled. "Here's where I tell you about doctor-patient confidentiality."

"I thought they were guests." Kenney answered back.

"Regardless, I can't get into specifics."

Copeland cursed under his breath. "Fine. He was sad when he got here. Three months ago, he was cured. Why?"

"No. Francis was fully recovered years ago. But he wasn't ready to leave. I tell all the guests that it's within their own power to leave. All they need to do is ask. Francis never asked. He stayed here willingly."

"And that didn't seem strange to you?" Kenney asked.

"On the contrary. People need to be ready to greet the world at their own pace, even if they've been emotionally healed."

Copeland put his foot on one of the benches that sat next to the front entrance. He stretched his leg out, working out a tight calf muscle. "So, Francis wasn't ready to leave until three months ago."

"No."

"Jesus, Dabney!"

"I'm sorry, Sheriff. Three months ago, Francis came into my office and requested to leave in three months' time. He said he'd finally found something to do. Something worthy of him leaving the sanitarium."

"Adam Parker." Copeland said.

Wendell shrugged. "He never mentioned him."

"When did he leave?" Copeland asked.

Wendell searched the recesses of his brain for the answer and found it. "About a week or so. Maybe ten days ago."

Kenney paced along the driveway. "Francis ever have any guests?"

"No."

"So, he paid the bill to stay here while being fully *healed*, as you say."

"The direct deposit payment came every month, so he remained."

Kenney rubbed the back of his head, looking for answers. But he kept digging up more questions. He looked to Copeland, who nodded. He felt the same.

"All right. We're going to need to look at your sporting equipment. I suspect we're going to find a missing 3-iron in the golf bag which also means I'm going to need to send a forensic team up here, Dabney."

"If you must, Sheriff. I just ask that you let me settle our guests before they arrive."

"Of course."

Wendell thanked him and headed back to the main house. Before entering the doors, Kenney called out. "Mr. Wendell. Would I be able to get a copy of your employee list for the time Francis was a guest here?"

"It'll take some time."

"Email it to Sheriff Copeland later. He can forward it to me."

Wendell waved goodbye and disappeared into the main house.

"What're you thinking?" Copeland asked Kenney.

"I don't know. Something. Anything."

"Solid police work."

"I try." Kenney smiled. "So, ten days ago he leaves, but three months ago he has this revelation that he needed to go."

"What happened three months ago?"

Kenney didn't need long to get there. "That was about the time when we had our incident with the Scout."

"That kid who tried to blow up the hotel? Homemade bomb, right?"

"Small atom bomb," Kenney corrected him and continued, "Parker was involved with that. If Francis had a bone to pick with Parker about something from their past, maybe seeing Adam on TV or reading about him in the news suddenly reminded Francis that he needed a score to settle."

Copeland took a moment to process. "Why ask to leave and then wait the three months?"

"To hatch a plan? Figure out how exactly to get Parker."

Copeland produced a phone from his jacket pocket. He scrolled through the contacts. "I'll get one of my boys up here to take you back to the station. Get you back to your car."

"I appreciate it, Sheriff."

"Just catch this guy. That way, I can close my murder case."

# Chapter 19
## Skateworld

In the 80s and mid-90s, most teenagers hung out at the mall or the local movie theater, but for many of the youth of Hilldale, the place to be was *Skateworld.* The roller-skating rink was still popular, even though the craze had passed it by. *Skateworld* was located in a corporate park. While today, the park still maintained a few companies, the section where *Skateworld* called home was run-down. It helped that the building was situated at the end of the long road that dispersed all members of the corporate park to their respective companies. You were able to avoid seeing the eye sore that *Skateworld* had become.

The building barely survived the years of abuse. The outside of *Skateworld* was boarded up and tagged with graffiti by various members of Hilldale's bored youth. The passage of time since *Skateworld* was opened also brought smashed-in windows, damaged walls and overgrown vegetation.

What little windows were left intact were tinted black and boarded up. The once large red letters spray-painted across the front façade of the building faded to a light pink. The lower portion of the '*e*' in *Skateworld* was so faded, it disappeared.

Adam, Becky and Nancy, backpack still slung over her shoulder, stood at where the front entrance used to be. It was covered in vegetation overgrowth that threatened to take over the parking lot next.

"Don't they have bum fights down here?" Nancy asked.

"Looking to place a bet?" Adam replied.

"Let's figure out a way to get inside," Becky said as she approached two large plywood boards covering what was once the front door.

Adam walked along the sidewalk that hooked around the side of the building, where the rest of the parking lot was laid out. A few windows, a bit taller than Adam's head were spaced out evenly along the wall. All the windows had plywood boards covering them.

He checked the boards. He pushed and pulled to find any signs of weakness. He found success with the third window he tried. The corner of the board was nailed into the wall, which had rotted from a water leak. The board was loose. Adam placed his fingers underneath the board and pulled. The board came off with ease. One it was removed, only the broken, grimy, tinted window remained.

Nancy was around the corner. She spotted Adam's success. She called back for Becky to join them. They tossed several large rocks through the window, clearing a semi-safe path through the broken glass.

Becky suggested, "Someone should climb in, open the front door for the other two."

Adam and Nancy looked to each other, then back to Becky. She realized what they were implying.

"Why me?"

"You suggested it," Adam said.

"You *can* volunteer."

"C'mon. You knew it would be you," Adam said to her.

Nancy nodded in agreement. "I'm more of the tech girl, not really an explorer. I'm better with heavy lifting."

"Heavy lifting!" Becky's face was red.

Nancy held up her hands. "Figure of speech, figure of speech." Nancy moved to the wall. She interlocked her hands for Becky to get a footing.

Becky begrudgingly backed up for a running start. Nancy readied herself. Becky raced at her. Arms pumping. She leapt into Nancy's hands, who pushed her up at the same time. Becky launched through the window with a crash. She shouted a few curse words, but nothing anyone on the outside could hear. Adam and Nancy were grateful for that.

"You good?" Adam shouted through the opened window.

"Yeah," Becky whined.

"Where are you?" Adam asked.

"Make-out corner."

Adam smiled. "Oh yeah. I remember that place." He turned to see Nancy who had a disgusted look on her face. "What? I'm not a creep."

Nancy didn't care to hear his case. She called out to Becky. "Meet you at the front door."

Nancy and Adam waited a few minutes for Becky to make her way through the darkness of the skating rink. Small talk was limited to remembrances of *Skateworld*, more pledges of non-creep actions on the part of the Adam and Nancy's lingering concern of the fate of her boyfriend.

The boards on the front door shook. Adam paused. Nancy took a step back. They shook again, this time moving slightly. The wood splintered along the bottom of one of the boards. They waited. Adam was about to call out, when the boards shuddered again. This time they fell over as the door from the inside swung open. Becky was in the doorway. Dust and sawdust in her hair. She coughed.

"We may need tetanus shots after this. It's pretty nasty in here."

Adam sniffed. "Smells lovely."

The stench came from the air vent directly over the entrance. Once they passed through the invisible wall of odor, the usual smell of mold and mildew remained. After a five-minute discussion as to what type of animal could've possibly died in the air vent, the investigation continued. The consensus was a giant rat, but no one would stick their head in the vent to verify. An unsolved mystery.

They stood in the middle of what was once the eating area of the skating center. To the right was the food service counter, kitchen in the back. If you walked around the counter, you'd find the arcade which consisted of twenty old style arcade machines.

To the left of the eating area were the lockers and bathrooms. Directly in front was the skating rink itself. They walked onto the wooden rink floor, smartphone flashlights leading the way. Nancy had her own tactical flashlight, which covered more space. Various mismatched pairs of roller skates laid across the rink floor.

"Last time I came here, it was high school," Adam said.

"It held on for another 10 years after that," Becky continued, "I was here one time during its last year. One of Caitlyn's friends had a birthday party. You could tell it was towards the end. Hardly anyone was here. One employee ran the concession stand and the lighting for the rink. It was pretty sad."

"So why *Skateworld*?" Nancy asked. "What'd you do here?"

"The usual. Skate. Hang out. Make out. Nothing different from any other normal teenager," Adam said.

"But we know that's not true. You're not normal. You were a bully." Becky said.

"Stop saying that. I wasn't."

"You kinda were," Nancy offered.

"And what messed up thing did you do to someone when you were here back in those high school days of yours?" Becky asked. She then added. "Particularly to this Francis kid."

Adam shrugged.

"He knows." Nancy wasn't fooled.

"Shut-up."

"Embarrassed?" Nancy asked.

"Maybe a little."

"Too bad," Becky moved closer to him, "We don't have the luxury of your hurt feelings."

"Dude. You were a dick back then and maybe a little now. We already know this. So just tell us." Nancy folded her arms. She leaned against a table, but quickly opted to stand when her hand touched the years of grime that had collected on the table-top.

Adam sighed. He pointed at the lockers. "It was during the Christmas break," he started.

* * *

*Skateworld* was alive and kicking, as kids of all ages ran around the eating area. Popcorn and peanut shells covered the dark-tones of the carpet which were worn down from years of abuse. The game room was abuzz with sounds of *Pac-Man*, *Galaga* and *Joust*. Old-style video games for the mid-90s, but still popular. Besides the owner of Skateworld couldn't be bothered to invest in new video games. Kids screaming. They were always screaming.

There was also screaming. Kids screaming. Chasing each other. Shouting obscenities. Parents chasing after them. More screaming. There was always screaming. Most of the younger kids kept to the eating area, game room and the skating rink. The older kids, the teenagers, floated from the game room to the rink and of course, to make-out corner.

A young Adam Parker sucked on the neck of a young girl. She was a junior and on the basketball team. She giggled, claiming he was tickling her. This quickly grew old for Adam, so he decided to ditch the junior year girl and make-out corner to find something else to do. He walked along the edge of the skating rink, laughing at the kids unable to stay on their feet. He especially enjoyed the multiple-person crashes. Those were always a favorite.

His interest piqued when he entered the game room and found Same Pants, playing a game of pinball by himself in the corner. He made a beeline for his favorite adolescent target and shoved himself on top of the pinball game, so Same Pants couldn't ignore him.

"Whatcha' doin', Same Pants?"

Francis said nothing.

"Don't ignore me. This will just get worse."

"What do you want?" Francis said out of the corner of his mouth.

"There you go. Just seeing how you're doing? Everything going all right?" Adam leaned back to check out Francis's pants. "Yup. I see we're sticking with the *Dockers* again."

"Please. Leave me alone," Francis pleaded.

"I'm bored, Same Pants. Let's do something fun."

"With me?"

"Sure. Why not?" Adam laughed.

"I'm fine right here." Francis focused on his game of pinball.

Out of the corner of his eye, Adam spotted two sophomore girls checking their new phones. An idea crept into his head and he went with it. He waved the girls over. They started talking, Adam being a senior added a lot of weight to his jokes and playful flirting.

He'd wrap his arm around Francis as he talked, as if they were best buds. A few jokes here and there, but not at Francis's expense. They were more like jokes with Francis. Like they were buddies.

And he never called him Same Pants once.

The flirting led to the inevitable walk to make-out corner. Adam leaned against the wall, while one of the girls kissed his neck. He never knew her name, nor did he care. His focus was on Francis who was seated at one of the circular couches, which doubled as a spot for kids to remove their skates.

Francis wasn't experienced in the ways of being intimate with a girl, something Adam had planned on. He watched as

Francis struggled with being close to the girl. She sat next to Francis and waited. And waited.

Adam called out from the wall, "Touch her, Same Pants." He laughed. He watched as Francis reached out and cupped the girl's breast. A wrong move.

The girl slapped Francis across the face and walked off in a huff. Adam laughed. Loud. It caught the attention of the other older kids in make-out corner. They all laughed at Francis. Tears formed in the corner of his eyes.

"Don't cry, Same Pants. You got to 2nd base!"

Francis ran off, into the skating rink. Adam kept laughing. Francis wasn't looking where he was running and a group of kids forming a chain with their hands undercut Francis and he flipped over. Landing on his back with a thud.

Adam roared with laughter. Falling to his knees in tears of joy.

Francis crawled away on all fours. His back sore. Desperate to escape the ridicule from everyone on the rink. They all had turned their attention to the freshman.

Adam couldn't stop laughing until he found the same junior year basketball player from earlier. She had watched with jealousy as Adam brought over the sophomore girl. He forgot about Francis and soothed the hoop star's anger with a few kisses on her cheek. Soon they were back to making out.

* * *

Adam stood in the middle of what was once make-out corner, now a distant memory and caked in mold. Becky and Nancy stood back from him. Each with their mouth agape at the story they just heard.

Adam turned around. "Yeah. I know."

"Where was he sitting?" Becky asked, trying to control the rage that boiled from within.

Adam pointed at the circular couch to Becky's side. He looked away, not wanting to make eye contact with her. Adam was always ashamed of his adolescence. When it was his little secret, he could chalk it up to being young, stupid and not knowing any better. But now, having to reveal it to his friends, he couldn't explain it away. He couldn't sugar coat what he was like. What he had done to others. Becky would think of him differently now. He couldn't blame her. She was right. He was a bully.

Becky ran her hands under the couch. She bent down and reached for something. Her hand came back with another envelope. *Clue #2* was scrawled on the front in black marker.

"Can we go now?" Nancy asked.

Becky followed her out, leaving Adam behind with his memories.

# Chapter 20
## Slushee Surprise

Not much to do when you're tied to a chair throughout the day except doze off, which is how Kevin spent most of the afternoon. After Francis forced him to recap one of his more traumatic memories from high school, he left the cabin. Kevin was alone.

He awoke from his nap some time later. Drool pooled in his lap. Not a highlight moment. He closed his mouth and shook his head to wake himself up. He glanced around the room. He was still in the living room, facing the window. Kevin, still bound to the chair, hopped closer to the window, careful to navigate around the couch.

He looked through the window. Still just the tops of trees. Kevin figured the cabin must be high up, but he couldn't make out any landmarks in the distance. *Maybe he wasn't in Hilldale*, he thought. A sound from outside startled him. It sounded like a gate shutting. And voices. He couldn't hop back to his original position in time, so he figured he'd just take whatever punishment was about to walk through the door.

The voices were closer. It sounded like two people. Kevin couldn't make out what they were saying, but he was certain it was two separate voices. Footsteps on the front porch. Key in the lock and the door opened.

Francis spotted Kevin's new position in the room. He smiled.

"Enjoying the view?"

Kevin smirked, grateful for not having to deal with any punishment.

Francis continued, "If you wanted to move closer, all you had to do was ask. I meant what I said before. I'm not your enemy."

"But you're going to kill me if Adam doesn't do what you ask."

Francis tossed the keys on the counter. He walked to the window. He leaned on it, making the forest his backdrop. "That's true. I did say that."

"Did you mean it?"

He paused. "I want to talk about Carson Owens again."

"Do we have to relive that again?"

"He tormented you the whole time he was in school. Two years."

"We've already been over this."

"I know." Francis folded his arms. "This is hard for you, I get that. What do you see when you look at me?"

Kevin stayed quiet. He shrugged.

A smile curled up from Francis's lips. "Be honest."

"C'mon," Kevin said. "Seriously?"

He clapped his hands and laughed. "Yes, please. What do you see?" Francis asked again.

Kevin took a deep breath. "A psycho. Someone who's holding on to a bad high school experience and has focused their anger towards one person. Blaming them for everything wrong in their life."

"Brilliant!"

"You're unhinged."

"Perhaps. There is special place in my rage-filled heart for Adam Parker. I spent many years after school in depression. I contemplated suicide. Even tried a few times. My last attempt is what had me put away for a bit. Away from society." He turned to face the window. Remembering back. "And there I remained, stewing in depressed thoughts, anger and confusion as to why my life was the way it was. How I became incapable of living in this world?"

Francis spun back around. The smile returned. "That's when I thought of where it all went wrong. That first day of school. By my lockers. Meeting Adam."

"It's just school. Everyone had a bully."

"Not Parker. Not Carson Owens."

"But I didn't want to kill Carson."

"Why is that?"

Kevin paused. "I don't know. He was gone after my sophomore year. I didn't have to deal with him. After school, I just had other friends. Adam."

"Parker was still your friend?"

"Always. Through all of it. He was my friend. We may not have hung out together for a while, but we were cool."

Francis smiled. He nodded, almost politely. "And I didn't have that? So that must be why I want Adam dead."

"Yeah. Maybe. I don't know. I think if you had some friends. You might not have not gone down this path."

"Friends like you had."

"Yeah."

Francis paused. "Carson Owens."

"I told you about him," Kevin broke eye contact.

"You told me about one incident with him. I want to hear about the other and before you deny it, I already know about it. I already know what happened, so spare me the usual excuse-laden speech."

Kevin was angry. He lifted up from his chair, only an inch, and slammed back down on the floor. "Why? What purpose does this serve?"

"Your delusion, Simpson!" Francis shouted in return. "You lecture me about taking the high road, like you. But you're on a path without the facts. You're living a life of ignorance, whether you know it or refuse to accept it."

"It was just high school!"

"Is that what you tell yourself when you're awake at night? When you're lying in bed, tormented with anxiety and searching for when you became this person? *It was just high school.*" Francis placed his hands on the chair rails and brought his face close to Kevin. "The next time I ask you about the other Carson Owens incident, you're going to tell me and then you're going to discover the truth."

"Truth about what?"

"Everything."

* * *

Adam finally rejoined Nancy and Becky, who were waiting for him beside the mini-van. He hoped the outside air washed away the stench and grime from the inside of *Skateworld.* At least he hoped it washed off. Becky held the envelope in her hand. Waiting for the right time.

Adam motioned to the envelope. "Well?"

She opened it and pulled out a piece of paper. She read aloud: "What's red, blue, green, yellow, black and pours all over?"

"Gross. Is this a dead baby joke? I hate those," Becky said.

"If it is, it's one I've never heard before," Adam said. He paced a bit, working out the clue in his head.

Nancy smiled. "I know this." Surprised at the blank stares. She looked to Adam, "You don't know this?"

"I'm not really up to date on dead baby jokes." Adam said.

"It's not a dead baby joke."

"Thank God," Becky muttered.

"It's a slushee machine. The frozen carbonated drink?"

"Seriously? Like *ICEE*" Becky asked.

"Yes. Just like it." Nancy nodded.

Adam agreed. "She's right. And I know which one Francis wants us to visit."

"Awesome. I can't wait for this story." Becky said, thick in sarcasm. She opened the driver side door.

"Thanks," Adam said. He didn't miss the sarcastic retort. "It's not in Hilldale. It's a *7-11* in South Haven."

"What'd you do?" Nancy asked.

"I'll tell you when we get there." Adam hopped in the back seat.

The city of South Haven is situated on the coastline of Connecticut. Interstate 95, a major thru-way from Boston to Florida, ran straight through South Haven. This made it easy to get to any part of South Haven. Just pick an exit from 40-43.

The *7-11* store that Adam had in mind was on the border of South Haven and New Haven, one of the more well-known cities in Connecticut by anyone who doesn't live in the state. When people think of Connecticut, it's typically high taxes first and then New Haven second, followed by Mystic Seaport.

The drive didn't take long and soon they found themselves standing in the potato chip aisle. Adam scanned the inside of the store, hoping to jog his memory of a Friday night so many years ago. While the store's layout changed, Adam remembered being in the corner of the store where the refrigerator with the beer was stocked. He was devising a plan to buy beer without being carded when the chime from the front door opening turned his attention and he spotted Francis.

"Adam. Are you even paying attention to me?" Becky called out. She snapped her fingers in his face, startling him from his daydream.

"Sorry. What?"

"What're you doing?"

"Trying to remember."

"And?" Becky asked.

\* \* \*

Adam spent the last fifteen minutes staring at the same 12-pack of beer. The cheapest one they had in the store. But he knew the clerk was on to him already. Twice, he called out asking if Adam needed any help. Adam refused. Politely. But he knew he was cooked.

The clerk wore the standard green and yellow button down short-sleeved company *7-11* shirt. The depressed fabric matched the look of disdain on the mid-20s, dark-skinned man's face as he attempted to validate his life inside of a convenience store. A life that he felt was meant of bigger things, but somehow was derailed.

From the corner of the store, Adam noticed the stains on the clerk's shirt. Also, that the clerk checked his flip-phone several times, as if waiting for someone to call to rescue him from this stalled portion of his life.

The chime to the front door sounded. It snapped Adam from his inductive trance. He quietly thanked the chime for that. Even though he had turned his back on being a detective, those instincts never stopped haunting him.

He looked to the door and noticed a familiar face. Francis was with a few friends. Adam didn't recognize them from school. But that didn't matter because Adam had an idea. A chance to get the beer and, more importantly, get it for free.

A young Francis and his friends hit the candy aisle hard. The clerk's attention was drawn to them as they tossed ring pops at each other.

"C'mon guys. Don't throw the pops." There was defeat in the clerk's voice.

The summer was exceptionally hot this time of year, so most kids wore tank-tops and shorts, including Francis. It was the first thing Adam noticed when he made his way to the candy aisle.

"Holy shit. Same Pants? Are you wearing shorts?"

Francis froze as soon as he heard Adam's voice. "Hey."

His friends quieted down. They knew about Adam.

"Candy, huh? You boys stocking up on sweets?"

Francis's friends didn't say anything. They kept their heads down.

"Shit. I ain't gonna bite. Same Pants been telling stories about me, I see."

"What do you want?" he asked.

"Why do you think I want anything? I saw you from the corner of the store. Wondered to myself: Why is Same Pants all the way in South Haven?"

"Why are *you* here?"

"I asked first," Adam replied.

"Camp. We're just getting something to eat before we head back."

"Like Friday the 13th type of camp?" Adam laughed.

"No, like boy scout camp."

Adam cackled. He slapped Francis on the shoulder with an opened hand. "I knew you were a boy scout. I just knew it."

He squirmed under the weight of Adam's hand. He looked to the floor, hoping this would end soon.

Adam was oblivious or didn't care. He continued, "So look, while you're here. I need a favor. I'm trying to buy some beer for tonight. Heading to a friend's house in town. But this guy behind the counter has been eye-balling me, so I doubt he'll let it slide. You know?"

He didn't look up. "What do you want?"

"I don't know. Something to distract him. Knock a display over. Get him to help you with something and I'll walk out with the beer."

Francis was quiet.

Adam grabbed a handful of candy from the rack. "I'll even swipe some of the candy with me for you. No charge."

The friends tugged on Francis's sweat-shirt. They nodded their ascent to Adam. Francis turned around and headed deeper into the store. Adam reached out and slapped him on the shoulder. "Atta boy, Same Pants."

He returned to the cooler and grabbed the beer. He headed straight for the counter. The clerk's gaze steadied on Adam as he approached with the case of beer in hand. The clerk recognized the walk of an underage kid attempting to buy beer.

Adam placed the case on the counter. He smiled and leaned in to read the nametag on the clerk's faded green shirt. "Hey Porter. How are you tonight?"

Porter didn't react. "All right."

"Indeed. How long have you worked here?"

"Why do you care?" Porter asked. Smirk on his face.

"It just seems like you'd rather be doing something else," Adam said. He spied Francis and his friends out of the corner of his eye. They stood at the slushee station. Each pouring frozen carbonated goodness into a cup.

"Look, I know what this is. You start being all nice to me. Trying to ease me into not asking you for I.D. because we both know you're nowhere near twenty-one. Am I right?"

Adam smiled. "Actually. I was trying to make this conversation look as casual as possible."

"And why's that?"

"Because the kids over at the slushee counter are trying to steal candy."

Porter stopped. He slow burned to Francis, who made eye contact with him. Instantly, Francis was nervous. He couldn't stop staring at Porter from across the store. Locked in a silent gaze.

Porter didn't look back to Adam. "Wait here a sec." He walked towards the slushee station, never breaking eye contact with Francis. He called out. "You boys think you're slick, huh?"

"What?" Francis asked. He looked to Adam, who smiled.

Adam waved and exited out the door. He heard the voice of Porter yelling for Francis to turn out his pockets and then he heard nothing else as he got into his car and drove away with the beer and some candy.

* * *

Nancy had an opened bag of potato chips in her hand. She quietly ate as Adam finished the story. "What happened to Francis?"

"I don't know. I never found out."

"And you never saw him after that?" Becky asked. She reached into the bag and popped a chip in her mouth. Crunching loudly.

"It was the summer between my 2nd and 3rd year of college. That fall, I went back and never really returned."

"I remember." Becky deadpanned.

Nancy pulled the bag taut and poured the crumbs into her mouth. Pieces of potato chips fell onto her shirt.

"Seriously?" Adam asked.

"I'm hungry." Nancy said.

"Did you even pay for those?"

"Yeah. When you were zoning out before. We're not all assholes."

"Reformed asshole," Adam corrected her.

"Eh." Becky wasn't buying it yet. "If you didn't see him after that, then this is it, right? This has to be the last clue."

Adam shook his head. "I don't know."

"So, now what?" Becky asked.

"We were sent here for a reason. I would think there's something else for us to find." Nancy said.

Adam looked around the store. Most of the layout had changed from what it once was so many years ago. The aisles used to be lined parallel to the counter, which made it easier to lift a snack-cake or glazed apple pie. The new perpendicular layout made more sense. All the aisles spilled out into the main area in front of the counter, where the current clerk, a middle-aged middle-eastern man, currently glared at them.

Adam smiled. The clerk did not return the gesture. He came around the counter. Marched down the aisle.

"What is this you're doing?" His English was broken, but not bad.

"Just remembering some things from the past."

"What that mean? I see you here talking and talking and only thing you buy were those chips that girl sucked down."

"Hey!" Nancy protested. "I didn't eat all of them."

"Sorry, we're just trying to remember something that happened here many years ago." Becky said.

"How long?"

Adam thought back, "Maybe around 2000. 2001."

The clerk nodded. "I remember this time."

"Seriously?" Nancy asked.

"Yes. That was my first year when purchased this store from my cousin. All the aisles were the wrong way. People could steal without being seen. I told him this constantly, but he never change."

Adam nodded profusely. "Yes."

The clerk ignored the outburst. "I buy store and before I can move shelves, I have robbery first week."

"Three kids?"

"Just one. He was arrested. I press charges."

"Do you remember his name?" Becky asked.

The clerk shook his head. "No. But he kept saying Parka. Parka. Parka. Like a coat, right?"

"Something like that." Adam said.

"Anyway, I fix shelves. No more theft. Well, not as much." The phone rang. He returned to the counter, mumbling about them leaving.

"You got him arrested, Adam." Becky said.

He protested. "That might not be the same incident."

"Sounds like it, Parka." Nancy said.

Adam looked at the slushee station, but everything was brand new. Nothing reminded him of that night. In fact, the only part of the store that remained relatively the same was the wall of glass-paneled refrigerators and freezers.

Probably much harder to renovate an entire refrigeration system when doing a remodel. Adam wagered a guess that it was probably cheaper to tear down the store and rebuild then shift all the refrigerators and freezers around. That's probably why they never changed. Even the beer was in the same location.

The beer.

"What kind of beer did you buy that night?" Becky had arrived at the same conclusion. She beat Adam to the punch, which slightly irked him. She recognized that fact as well. "Get over it."

"Fine. It was the cheapest beer of the day. Natty Light."

"It's still the cheapest," Nancy replied.

"Classics die hard." Adam agreed.

They made their way to the corner refrigerator. Natural Light, every college student's top choice for its inexpensive pricing and beer-like taste, was on the lower shelf.

Becky pulled out the first 12-pack. Nothing. She reached in and grabbed a few more, until she found a taped envelope to the back of one of the cases. She handed it to Adam.

He ripped open the envelope to find one sheet of loose-leaf paper, tattered edges where it was ripped from the notebook. On it was a simple message, scrawled in blue ink.

"Well?" Becky demanded.

Adam flipped the note around to show her. *The end and the beginning.*

"What's that mean?" Becky asked.

"Where this all started," Adam said.

# Chapter 21
## Connect the Dots

If the trip to Brookville enlightened Kenney on anything to do with the threat against Parker, it was that he was nowhere closer to the truth now than when this all started. Normally a case like this would be assigned to one of his detectives, but Kenney didn't want to saddle any of his officers with a case involving Parker. Most of them didn't like Parker anyway.

Typically, the police don't like helping private detectives. They were considered less-than in many official law enforcement circles, but Kenney gave plenty of leeway to Parker and friends. No one really knew why. People called Kenney soft when it came to Parker. He knew he had a blind-spot toward the former kid detective. Growing up, all Parker wanted to do was stop bad guys. When Kenney first started on the force, his countless run-ins with the kid detective agency was infuriating. But over time, he admired Parker's resolve in trying to make the town and the world a better place.

Kenney wasn't going to force his officers to take lead on the case. Parker, for better or worse, was his responsibility and he needed to see it through. But after banging his head against the wall in Brookville, there wasn't much space to go anywhere else.

All Sheriff Copeland cared about were his own townspeople, something Kenney understood, even if he didn't agree with ignoring anyone who wasn't from Brookville. Oliver Francis may have been a Hilldale resident once, but his anger for Parker developed at the Brookville Sanitarium and that *was* on Copeland's watch. Kenney expected more help from his counterpart, but he was getting nothing as he drove past the sign wishing him well as he left Brookville.

The kidnapping of Kevin Simpson, the murder of his two officers, the killing of Thompson required a lot of planning and a massive amount of leg work. One man, three months removed from a place where he already claimed to have been healed, but not ready to join society. Friends with the staff. First name basis with everyone. Kenney wasn't buying it. Francis had help and his hunch was that it was someone on the staff.

After returning from his road trip, Kenney sat in his office for over an hour. He watched the stationhouse from behind his desk. His office had several windows, which allowed Kenney easy sightlines on all the coming and goings of his officers. He watched detectives working other cases. Shift changes. Several of his officers noticed their boss keeping an eye on them, so they found work to do. To keep busy. Kenney noticed this as well. It was amusing to him seeing the confused looks of his officers simply caused by his own blank stares.

The phone rang. Kenney grabbed it before the first ring ended. He barked his greeting. "Yeah." He waited for the response. "I'll be right there."

He was in his car five minutes later. Thoughts of the girl at *Lonnie's Tavern.* What had she heard and when? Who said it? Where? The phone call was the hospital. She was awake and talking. Kenney needed a break in the case and he was hoping Jane Doe would provide it.

* * *

He was greeted at the elevator by the protection detail he had assigned. They griped about their relief being late again, but Kenney didn't have the time nor the want to discuss this with them. He brushed it off and promised to address it tomorrow, when in reality he had no intention of doing that. He had a case to solve.

Before he entered Jane Doe's room, a doctor stood in his way. It was one of the many doctors who attended to Jane Doe. She was not smiling. He noticed her red hair and the freckles on her cheeks to match, although he didn't know why that was important.

"Can I help you, Captain?" She held her arm out, blocking his path.

"I hear she's awake."

"Yes. And we're making sure she stays awake. She can't have visitors."

"I'm not a visitor. I'm the police."

She chuckled, not because it was funny, but because she found him ignorant. "You're not talking to her."

Kenney took a deep breath, attempting to control the rage that was mounting inside of him. "Who are you?"

"Doctor Charlotte Rawlings." She tapped the nametag on her white coat.

Kenney noticed her red hair again. He shook it off. "Look, Doctor Rawlings. I've got a civilian whose life may be in danger and this girl is my only lead."

"Now, you look," she jabbed her finger in his chest. "I have a patient whose life *is* in danger and I'm not going to let you upset her and possibly complicate her recovery."

"First. That hurt," he rubbed the spot on his chest where her finger stabbed him. "Second. Recovery from what?"

"She has been off her meds for quite some time."

"What kind of medication? For what?" Kenney asked.

"I'm not at liberty to say."

"Listen, lady…"

Rawlings corrected him, "Doctor."

"Listen, doc. I'm the police. You understand that. You're at liberty to tell me everything."

"Wow," Rawlings laughed. "You're not a very smart cop, are you? And not the first moron in blue I've had to deal with today."

Kenney fumed. "Where do you get...wait. What other moron, I mean, cop did you have to deal with?"

"Sheriff Copeland. From Brookville. He's coming down with a Mr. Wendell to pick her up."

"She's a patient from the sanitarium?" Kenney asked.

"Seems so. Escaped, I would think."

Kenney's mind raced. A connection between Francis and Jane Doe. He needed to know more. "I need to ask her a few questions and I'm really not in the mood to argue with you."

Rawlings paused. She didn't like to lose. Not in her own hospital. She compromised. "I'm going in with you."

"Fine."

She opened the door and walked past Kenney, who caught a whiff of a floral scent wondering why he cared that he enjoyed it so much.

The room was quiet, compared to the hallway. No nurses walking from room to room. No phones ringing. The only noise was the beep of the monitor and the machinations of the IV drip.

There was a nurse by the bed reading her vitals, but she exited as soon as Kenney cleared his throat. Rawlings apologized and thanked the nurse, all the while tossing the mean-eye to Kenney. He didn't care.

The girl looked at Kenney but said nothing.

"How are you feeling?" He asked.

She shrugged. "Fine."

"We didn't find an I.D. on you."

"Gloria. Gloria Hicks."

Rawlings said, "Dr. Wendell confirmed this over the phone."

"Doctor Wendell is coming?" Hicks asked.

"Yes, dear. They're going to take you back to Brookville."

"Is Ollie with him?" She smiled. Her cheeks reddened with embarrassment. "He says we're not boyfriend and girlfriend, but I think he likes me and he's afraid to show it."

"To show it to who? The doctor?"

She nodded.

"Anyone else?"

Hicks was quiet. Her smile remained. She made circles in her hair with her finger. She hummed a song that Kenney didn't recognize. He waited for more information, but Hicks wasn't interested in answering.

"What's the last thing you remember?" Kenney asked.

"I was in a dirty restaurant. Drinking soda. Then I was in some place cold and wet. My soda was gone."

"Who were you with? Was Ollie with you?"

She smiled. "I'm not supposed to say."

"Was it just you two?"

"I'm not supposed to say!" She screamed.

Rawlings stepped in, "All right, Chief Kenney. That's enough."

He ignored the doctor's orders and continued, "Do you know Adam Parker?"

"Adam Parker is next." She giggled like a kid giddy with excitement. "Adam Parker is next." The giggling grew louder, longer, until it was full-blown laughter. "Adam Parker is next! Adam Parker is next!"

"Are we done?" Rawlings spoke up, over the laughter.

Kenney nodded. "Yeah, we're done." He left the room.

Rawlings followed, but not before calling the nurses over with a sedative for Hicks. The nurse raced by and entered the room, the laughter subsided once the door shut behind the nurse.

Rawlings offered, "Sorry, she wasn't more helpful. But I warned you."

"Yeah, well. I'm not surprised. What kind of insane is she?"

Rawlings paused. "You are extremely untactful, you know that?"

"I've been called worst. Please, doc. What's her deal? Before the Brookville sheriff shows up and takes away my only lead."

She took a breath. Weighing her decision. "She's bi-polar with symptoms of schizophrenia."

"Jesus."

"I'm guessing she escaped from the sanitarium with some of her meds, but once she ran out, she slowly deteriorated into the girl you found in the basement of that dive bar." Rawlings continued, "We have her on some stuff now, but nothing like her prescribed amount."

"What'll happen to her?"

"The same thing that happens to all patients who are sent to the Brookville Sanitarium. She'll be forgotten."

Kenney noticed the look of sadness in her eyes. "You've been to the place, huh?"

"I did a brief residency there during med school. I've never returned." Rawlings nodded a goodbye and returned to the room to see to the girl. The laughter had died down when the door opened.

Kenney left for the elevators, not really sure where he was going, but he knew he had the makings of a lead.

* * *

Kenney leaned on his car. He stared at the neon sign for *Lonnie's Tavern.* It was busted. The glass was cracked on the last half of *Tavern,* so when the neon was turned on it read *Lonnie's Tav.* Kenney thought it seemed appropriate given the state inside the bar. Calling it a dive was being generous.

After leaving the hospital, Kenney instinctively drove straight to *Lonnie's.* The conversation with Gloria Hicks confirmed his suspicion that the bar had more to offer to the case. *Lonnie's* was a staple of Hilldale, but not in a good way. Along with the damaged sign, the façade was stained with rust from rainwater that poured from a broken gutter atop the roof. The gutter hadn't been fixed for quite some time, going on seven years now.

Kenney titled his head to follow the reddish-brown stain that marked the entire front of the building. A long, slanted line of rust led from one side of the building to the other where it stopped at the entrance to the alley that ran along the side of the building. He pushed himself off the car and walked towards the alley as if following the rust-stained arrow.

There were several lights along the alley, one situated over the side entrance to the bar. It highlighted the alley's layout which was a paved strip leading to two dumpsters at the end of the alley. A fence ran the length of the alley opposite the building. Kenney had one thought on his mind as he walked the length of the alley.

The girl. Jane Doe. Gloria Hicks. What did she hear? Who said it? Who drugged her? Was she drugged?

He unlatched the flashlight from his belt and scanned the base of the alley. He brought the light to the side of the building and shined it on the side door entrance. No doubt a way to empty the trash and empty beer bottles into the dumpsters.

Kenney glanced behind the dumpsters but found nothing except trash and a scurrying rat. The rat ran under the adjacent fence. It was an easy getaway, as the bottom of the fence was chewed up from years of disuse. He followed the rodent's escape path, peering over the wooden fence. The fence was grimy to the touch. He guessed it had never been cleaned since it was installed. Thinking back, Kenney wondered if this was the same fence they had back when he first walked the Hilldale beat. It wouldn't surprise him.

The other side of the fence was in contrast to what the alley had to offer. A garden laced with a babbling brook of water and brightly-colored flowers that Kenney had never seen before. He ran his hand along the fence, trying to ignore the years of dirt. He found a loose board. Then another and another. Three boards, all loose and yet, attached to each other. This was a gate. A quickly-made gate meant for a quick passage between the alley and the garden. But more importantly, a gate meant for only those who knew about it. He pushed the boards aside and walked into the garden.

There was a building on the other side of the garden. A large neon shrimp on top, backwards as Kenney faced it, but he knew where he was standing. The backyard of the *Slammin' Sushi.* It was no great revelation that the *Slammin'* Sushi shared a fence with *Lonnie's Tavern*, but the makeshift gate gave Kenney pause.

He spotted another building tucked away at the corner of the garden. Bigger than a shed, although it could be with the amount of upkeep that this garden needed. The outside of the shed was decorated like a cabin. There was a path that led straight to the front door. Kenney took it. He stood at the door. Listening for voices. He brushed his hip with his hand, unclasping the leathered lock of his holstered sidearm.

He placed his left hand on the door, while steadying his right hand on the gun, still on his hip. He pushed slowly to make sure the door was unlocked and open. It was. He shoved the door and charged into the cabin. Gun in hand, as he raised it up.

The inside of the cabin was dark. Kenney made out the outline of the furniture, but nothing else. He fumbled for a light switch near the door. He clicked it on. The room lit up. To the left was a kitchen area. A living room to the right, where a couch and chair sat. There was a window, but no view. A white screen rested behind several panes of glass.

Kenney walked closer. He studied the wall. A window to nowhere. As he leaned on the wall, he felt a switch behind the drapes. He flipped it and the wall exploded with light.

The view of a forest stretched out in front of him from behind the window. He couldn't make out where the stretch of trees was located, but he figured it didn't matter, as long as it seemed like the cabin was somewhere else and not in the backyard of a sushi restaurant. He spotted a metal folding chair sitting on the other side of the couch. He didn't notice it when he first entered the cabin. If he had, he would've headed straight for it on account of the cut pieces of duct tape and rope tied to the chair.

He spoke under his breath. "Simpson."

He suddenly realized where he was standing. He found Kevin, but he wasn't here anymore. If not, where? And why move him now? Unless Adam was done with that ridiculous game. If that's the case, then this was ending, and Kenney had no idea where to look.

He flipped open his phone. He dialed Adam. It went straight to voicemail. He tried Becky next. Straight to voicemail.

"Dammit!"

He stopped himself from tossing the phone. Part of the reason he had the flip phone was because of an ill-advised phone toss after learning of an officer's poor decision-making skills. Instead, he pocketed the phone with some force.

He exited the cabin. He stood in the garden, hoping for inspiration to strike. He spotted an older, Asian man watching him from inside the *Slammin' Sushi*. The man hid as soon as Kenney made eye contact with him, but it was too late. Kenney made his way to the restaurant. He needed to find Adam and Kevin. It was time to end this.

# Chapter 22
## At the Lockers

It was getting late. The minivan had been parked in the Hilldale High School parking lot for thirty minutes. Adam and Nancy waited inside the car, as Becky was outside talking to her husband on the phone. Several times, Becky raised her voice, but this time Adam wasn't concerned. He was no longer worried about Becky's marriage. He sensed a finality to this case, no matter the outcome. He knew Becky was hiding her decision to quit playing detective with them. He couldn't find fault with her logic. Family does come first.

What Adam didn't anticipate was the family that the agency provided him. When he returned to Hilldale four months ago, he was not in a good place and Kevin and Becky were there to help him. Almost immediately, Adam's crush for Becky returned and he was terrible at hiding it. But now, those feelings, while still of love, are only of that for a great friend. In fact, this whole ordeal with Francis superseded any latent feelings Adam had for Becky. He cared for Becky, but not as he did all those years ago when he developed his crush. Becky was his friend, one of his best friends and to see her in pain over being part of the agency was something that Adam couldn't stand.

He was waiting for Becky to tell him, but he already knew. She was quitting. Adam would have to move on without her, hopefully, not to his death, but moving on to something that included stopping Francis from his ill intentions.

Nancy fidgeted in the passenger seat. Her legs up on the dashboard as she nervously bit her nails. She worked on the fingernails of her left hand after biting all the nails on her right hand down to the nubs. Adam watched her carefully. For some reason, he wasn't nervous about Kevin. Francis's anger and rage were directed at him, not Kevin. His friend was merely the means to get him to go down memory lane. A trip that revealed Adam's former self to be less-than.

"Don't be nervous," Adam offered. His phone vibrated in his pocket. He checked the caller I.D. and quickly tapped the button to send it to voicemail.

Nancy spun around. "Are you serious?"

"I'm don't think Kevin is in danger."

"This guy is a madman."

"Francis is angry at me. He blames me for his life. Holding Kevin is to make sure I go through with this whole charade."

"And at the end of this, he's just going to let him go?"

"Yes, I think so."

"And you?"

"Probably kill me."

Nancy paused. She didn't know what to say.

"...which I'm hoping to avoid. Jesus, Nancy. You want me dead?" Adam said, half-laughing.

"No. You just seem so flippant about it."

"I'm not. I don't want to die."

"Then we should do something about that, don't you think? Aren't you formulating a plan?"

"Nothing is coming to mind. We walk in. He lets Kevin go. And then...nothing. I got nothing after that."

"I wish you had let me stop at the house."

"You're not getting any guns. Bringing more guns isn't the answer."

"It's *an* answer. Not your answer."

The side door slides open. Becky is off the phone. "Did Kenney call you?"

"He tried, but I don't have time right now."

"It might be about Kevin."

"I'm pretty sure Kevin is inside." He jabbed his thumb towards the school.

Becky ignored him. "And why is there yelling in here?"

Nancy said, "Parker doesn't have a plan. And he won't let me get my gun."

"We don't need more guns," Becky replied.

"That's what I said." Adam flicked his hands up, signaling that he was right.

Nancy made a face at him. "Look. It's my boyfriend in there. And I'm going to make sure he comes out alive."

"We all are," Adam said. "That's why me going in there, getting Kevin away from him and giving myself to Francis is the best plan we have."

"Giving yourself?" Becky asked.

"Adam is planning on dying," Nancy answered.

"I didn't say that. I just don't have a plan for when I trade places with Kevin."

"Then you're planning on dying, Adam." Becky said. "That's pretty much what you're doing."

"Again," Nancy suggested. "Let me get my guns."

"And what's that plan look like?" Adam asked her. His tone increased. "What's your big idea with the guns? You come in. Pull your gun. Demand Kevin be handed over to you? Then Francis pulls his gun. Puts it to Kevin's head and tells you to drop yours and slide it over to him. Then what do you do?" Before she can answer, Adam continued. "I'll tell you. You'll do exactly what he says. You'll drop your gun and slide it over to him. Why? For the very same reason you want to get your gun. Love. Because you love him. You'll do anything to save him and that's going to include giving Francis two guns. So, no, your plan is not going to work the way you think it will." He charged out of the mini-van, angry for blowing up.

He could hear Nancy crying in the car. Becky turned to Adam. "That was harsh."

"I know."

Adam looked to the school. Empty, as it should be at this time of night. But Adam knew Francis was in there. Waiting for him. Waiting to end it all. Adam was ready to oblige him. Whatever the outcome.

"How's Mark?" Adam asked.

"I don't really think this is a good time."

"C'mon, Becky. Is there ever a good time?"

"I suppose." She smiled. "He's good. Just worried."

The passenger door opened. Nancy walked around the front of the mini-van and joined them. "I'm sorry."

"No, I'm sorry. I shouldn't have yelled." Adam said.

"I just don't know what else to do."

"Look, I care about Kevin, too. The only way to do this is to go in there and see how it plays out. Once Kevin is handed over. You and Becky leave with him and I'll stay."

"And you'll be killed," Becky said.

"It's the only way."

"Dammit, Adam!" She punched him in the arm. Hard. He winced. "You dying isn't the answer."

Adam smirked. ""It's *an* answer. Not your answer." He smiled at Nancy. She smiled back, recognizing her own words being repeated.

* * *

Any building that's intended purpose is to be filled with people, always has a soothing calmness when empty. Hilldale High was positively serene when they walked through the broken front door. Adam noticed the damaged lock when they pulled into the parking lot, furthering his belief that they were not first to arrive at the school.

When Adam attended school, he enjoyed the quietness of the hallways. He'd walk the halls in the early mornings after being dropped off by his mother. The squeak of his shoes on the recently-mopped tile floors, the muffled voices of people in rooms, the faint sounds of teachers preparing for their day would bring him ease.

Tonight reminded Adam of those moments, but the anticipation of what was to come shaded any fond remembrances. No lights were on inside the school. Only the large halogen bulbs of the parking lot lamps provided illumination via the school windows. The outside lights were enough to get around the corridors, even the ones left in shadow.

They walked down the main hallway in silence. Nancy and Becky followed Adam, as he led them to the only location where he knew Francis would be waiting. Their old lockers. To Adam, it was only a memory of time past, but for Francis it was the beginning of his own personal hell. Adam felt a multitude of emotions over the past few days – confusion, fear, anger, but most importantly – guilt.

Guilt for the type of person he was back in school and maybe for the type of man he was now. Did he learn anything? Did he understand his actions? The look on Becky's face after the revelations of his adolescence was like a knife to his soul. He was pained, but instead of understanding the pain, he spiraled into a depression. He was depressed. Depressed from the guilt.

 The walk to his old locker didn't scare him nearly as much as it should, even though he expected to be killed. He felt like he deserved it. This wasn't courage. It was acceptance.

They came to the stairs that led to the second floor. Becky grabbed his arm. Adam turned to face the tears in her eyes.

"Are you sure about this?" She asked.

"There's no other way. We need to get Kevin."

Becky slid her hand from Adam's arm to his hand. She squeezed. Adam squeezed back. "Stop trying to make me cry."

She laughed. It helped with her nerves, but not by much.

Nancy watched it all, not saying a word. She ached for Kevin. To hold him in her arms and be together, away from all this danger.

Adam nodded. He ascended the stairs. The women followed.

As they stepped onto the second floor, the air was different. Adam sensed the presence of others. He paused. He closed his eyes and listened for the sounds of breathing.

"No funny business, Parker. I've got your friend here."

Adam's eyes shot open. He expected Francis to be waiting. He walked the hallway and rounded the corner to find Francis and Kevin standing in front of the lockers. The very same locker that Francis used all those years ago. He held a gun to Kevin's temple. Kevin remained still. Sweat down his forehead. He nodded at Adam. "Hey."

"Hey," replied Adam.

Nancy, upon seeing Kevin's predicament, took a step towards him. Francis responded by digging the muzzle of the gun deeper into the side of Kevin's head. "Careful now. Keep your cool and you'll have your boyfriend back."

Kevin muttered. "We're not boyfriend and girlfriend."

"Like hell we're not, Simpson." Nancy gritted through her clenched teeth.

Kevin wanted to smile, but he remembered the gun. "Now, you tell me."

"Enough," Francis said.

"I did what you asked. I went to those places. I told the stories." Adam said.

"And?"

"And what? We all know what kind of person I was. I wasn't a saint. I'm sorry that I bullied you. I'm sorry that I turned your life into this horrible mess."

"Not just me, Parker."

"I know. Isn't that what this is all about? To learn how shitty of a person I was or still am."

Francis pointed the gun at Adam, "Now, don't go getting all depressed and whiny about your life. If I never came along, you wouldn't have given it a second thought about what you were. Only now, that I've forced you to see the type of person you were, you've become self-reflective. I'm not sorry you feel bad. It's been one day. I've been horribly scarred for my whole life!"

"So, I'm here now. Let Kevin go. Then do what you want with me."

"More."

"What do you mean?" Becky asked.

"I mean, I'm not done with Parker yet."

"Fine! Just let Kevin go." Adam shouted.

Francis smiled. "Me and Simpson had a nice little chat while you were running around town." He tapped the gun on Kevin's head. "Didn't we?"

"C'mon, man. Just get it over with." Kevin pleaded.

"Yeah, we talked about school. We talked about our experiences. Our shared experiences, if you will." Francis smiled. He studied Adam's face and waited for the look of confusion to appear. Once it did, he continued, "Simpson told me something interesting. He said you two didn't really hang out in high school."

"I guess not. We travelled in different circles."

"Be fair, Parker. You wanted to be popular and people like Simpson and me, we're just never going to be those guys."

"Ok. Yes. High school sucks. We get it."

"No! You don't! High school is only the beginning! It's where we're classified into groups. Nerds, geeks, jocks, losers, potheads! It all starts in high school."

Nancy stepped forward. "That's ridiculous. You change. You grow up. You mature."

"Keep telling yourself that. And after this is over, think about who you are. The person you became. The things you like. The people you hang out with. Think of all that. And then think about where you developed those tastes. You'd be surprised."

"Get to the point." Adam demanded.

"Fine. Who'd you hang out with in high school, Parker?" Francis shoved Kevin forward, creating space between them. The gun was now trained on the back of Kevin's neck.

"I don't remember."

"Yes, you do."

Adam didn't know where Francis was going, but stalling wasn't working. "I guess, a couple of guys on the football team. Whoever was throwing a party."

"Carson Owens?"

Kevin reacted to the familiar name. He looked to Adam for a response, more interested in the reply than everyone in the hallway.

"Yeah, I guess. Why?"

Francis grinned. Slowly curling his lips, as if holding on to a deep, dark secret, which is exactly what he was doing. "Kevin. You knew Owens, right?"

"You know I did." Kevin said. He stared at Adam.

"What?" Adam asked. He was confused.

"You see Parker, your friend here was under the impression that during high school, while you were terrorizing people like me, you left him alone. Out of some sense of loyalty."

Becky looked to Adam. "Adam, what's he talking about?"

Adam ignored her. He listened to Francis, while maintaining eye contact with Kevin. He knew where Francis was going. "It was a long time ago," he said to Kevin.

"What's he talking about?" Kevin asked.

"Simpson. Tell Adam what you told me. Tell him about your most memorable encounter with Carson Owens."

"C'mon. Not here."

"Yes! Here!"

Becky asked again. "What's he talking about, Adam?"

"It was high school you whiny little bitch!" Adam yelled at Francis. "Jesus Christ! Let him go!"

"No! Not until you're ruined! Not until these friendships based on lies are exposed. Not until you understand what it truly feels like to be alone and hated!" Francis screamed. Gun shaking in his hand.

"Adam!" Becky screamed.

Francis trained the gun on Nancy. "Tell them, Simpson. Tell them or I kill your girlfriend. Right here in front of you. Her blood splattered all over the school lockers."

Kevin screamed. "All right!" He gathered himself. The hallway was quiet, awaiting the story. "Freshman year..."

"Stop," Adam said. "I was there."

"What?"

"I was there. In the locker room. I was there that day," Adam admitted.

Kevin froze. His hands shook. He forgot about the gun pointed at Nancy. He forgot about the situation. The life or death peril they were all in. He focused on his friend. "You knew?"

Adam nodded. "I'm sorry, Kev. I really am."

"Not yet, you're not." Francis added. He turned his head to the shadows behind him. "Bring him out!"

Everyone looked beyond Francis, towards the darkness. The shadows moved. Two figures emerged. One tall, slender and familiar. Jeff Tanaka walked behind another man. He held him tight. The man was heavier than he was when Adam last saw him. He bled from his lip. A bruised eye. The heavy-set man clutched his arm, like it was broken.

Carson Owens looked at everyone in the hallway, not sure what to do.

"Parker?"

# Chapter 23
## The Truth

Kevin whipped his head around at the sound of Adam's name. He noticed the heavy-set. He didn't recognize the face of the man that many years ago made his school life hell when they were younger. It didn't click until Adam replied back.

"Hey Carson." Adam said. He then nodded towards Tanaka. "I was wondering when you'd get here."

"Ha! You didn't know Jeff Tanaka was with me. Knock it off!" Francis contested.

"I knew you had help," Adam said. "My guess was Jeff. All the stories you made me revisit. They were all about you. All of them except the night of the party. The night of Tanaka-Bomb."

"Let's get this over with." Tanaka finally broke his silence. He was angry at the reminder of that night many years ago.

Adam smirked. "So, you haven't forgiven me after all, have you, Jeff?"

"I'll never forgive you." Tanaka squeezed Owens' shoulder out of instinct, channeling his hatred for Parker into his grasp.

Owens winced. "Listen, I'm not sure what's going, but why am I here, exactly?" He continued to sweat. He spotted the rest of the people in the hallway. "Becky Wilson?"

Becky held up her hand in a frozen wave. "Hey Carson."

"What's going on?" Owens asked.

"Shall I continue, Parker? Or would you like to take the honor?" Francis asked.

Adam seethed. He hadn't expected Carson. He looked to Kevin again. "None of this matters."

Francis laughed. "Keep telling yourself that. Look at your so-called best friend's face. He begs to differ."

Memories flooded back for Kevin. Owens in the hallway every day taunting him. Owens laughing at him. Calling him names at lunch. The locker room. He tried to remember if Adam was with him. Ever. "You hung out with Carson?"

Adam said, "We were in the same circles, yes."

Francis motioned for Tanaka to act and he did. He pushed Owens in the back. Hard. "Tell them," he barked.

"Look. I'm sorry. I don't even remember a lot of high school. I know I was a dick, but... OW!" Tanaka punched him in the back. A shot to the kidney. Owens doubled over.

"No one is here for your apology. We're here for the truth!" Francis shouted. "Now spill it!"

Owens hesitated. The hallway was quiet, waiting for Owens. Nancy wiped away tears from her eyes. Seeing Kevin with a gun to his head was tearing at her normally cool and collected resolve. Kevin saw her reaction. He bowed his head.

Kevin said, "Say what you have to say, Carson."

Tanaka grabbed Owens, still doubled over on the floor, and yanked him up. "Talk!"

Kevin looked to Owens. He waited. Owens took a breath. He looked to Francis, who waved the gun again. He looked at Adam. "Sorry."

\* \* \*

It was the end of summer. About one week before senior year was set to begin and Adam wanted nothing to do with it. He was having the best summer of his life. He was out every other night with most of the football team, including Owens. He met a lot of girls and even spent a weekend in Key West with his new friends.

Tonight, was the rare occasion where the party was at Adam's house, as his mother picked up another night shift and left Adam to his own devices for the night. That meant party. It only took a few phone calls to get most of the football team's starting squad over his house, along with a few other dozen or so partygoers.

Old enough to party, but not old enough to drink didn't stop Adam. He was more than a few beers passed his limit which meant everything that was suggested to him was a 'great idea'.

"Adam! Let's do a keg stand!"

"Great idea!"

"Adam! Can we use your mom's bedroom?"

"Great idea!"

"Yo! Parker! I lit the backyard on fire!"

"Great idea!"

Adam sat on the front steps of his house. He spied the Wilson house when Owens opened the front door and took a seat alongside him.

"That cute girl, Becky Wilson lives next door, right?" Owens asked.

"Yeah. She's in college now."

"Didn't you hang with her? When you were younger?"

"That was a long time ago."

"Damn," Owens shoulder-bumped him. "Ever tap that?"

Adam laughed. "I was 10."

"So?"

Another laugh. Owens took a swig of his beer. He belched. More laughter from Adam.

"Which house is Simpson's?"

Adam pointed across the street. The faded green house was dark except the front porch light.

"You guys were friends, too?"

Adam shrugged. "Sort of. We played together."

"You played detective. C'mon. Everyone knows about that stuff." Owens shoved him again. "I'd always see your name in the paper. Thought you were cool."

"Seriously?"

"Then I met you. Ha!" Owens punched him on the arm.

Adam rubbed the sore. "Thanks. Anyway, that was a long time ago."

"Want to have some fun?"

"Always," Adam pounded the rest of his beer.

"Which neighbor of yours has a dog?" Owens asked.

Adam paused. He tried to figure out why Owen wanted to know that, but then he tried to remember who on his street actually had a dog.

Initially, Adam didn't like the idea after Owens explained his plan, but the beers in his system created a low tolerance for bad decisions, which led to Adam situated behind a parked car in front of Kevin's house as Owens collected several pounds of dog poop from the neighbor's yard.

Owens joined Adam behind the car. He shoved a paper-bag full of poop into Adam's chest. "You're up."

"Me?"

"Yeah, you. I went and picked up the dog shit. I got some of it on my hands. My shoes. My socks." Owens examined his pant leg. "My jeans. Dammit. What the hell was I doing?"

Adam shook his head. He stifled a laugh to avoid detection. They ducked behind the car again. Owens nudged Adam with his shoulder. "Go."

"It's not lit, yet."

"You sure about that?" Owens asked. Smile across his face.

Adam looked to the bag, which glowed in his hand. The fire grew. Adam broke from the car. He ran to front door of Kevin's house and dropped the flaming bag of dog poo.

He rang the doorbell and ran. He returned to his original hiding spot behind the car with Owens. They waited. The door opened and a younger Henry Simpson, Kevin's father, appeared. The confusion on his face quickly turned to panic when he noticed the fire on his front porch.

His reaction was immediate. He stomped on the bag to put out the flames. He didn't realize what the bag contained. He stomped over and over. The fire continued to burn. He lifted his foot up for another stomp. The bag stuck to his foot. His shoe ignited in flames. Henry shrieked.

Owens was beside himself with laughter. He pulled on Adam's shirt in his laughing fit, but Adam was not laughing. He was embarrassed. Ashamed. He watched his friend's father, the man who was a surrogate father to Adam at times when he was younger, being played for a fool. And even worse, it was Adam's fault.

Henry kicked his foot forward to shake the flaming bag loose. It worked. It sailed in the air, like a fiery comet; catching in the branches of the small dogwood tree in the front yard. Instantly, the tree caught fire. Henry shrieked again. He ran from the front porch to the side of his house. Seeking the water hose.

Adam took the opportunity and ran from his hiding place. He returned to his home. Owens was right behind him, laughing the whole way. Once they made it inside the house, through the front door, Adam stood at his front window. He had to shove through the entire party of on-lookers who were all laughing at what they witnessed.

Henry came from the side of his house, green garden hose in his hand. He blasted the tree with a stream of water. It did nothing to control the blaze.

Everyone from inside the Adam's house, behind the windows cheered on the efforts of Kevin's father. Adam watched in horror, ashamed of what he had done. Embarrassed. Owens grabbed him around the shoulders, screaming how beautiful it was.

Adam smiled.

* * *

The hallway was silent. Owens finished the story.

Francis giggled and put his arms around Kevin. "Tell me again how Adam respected your friendship."

"I'm so sorry, Kevin." Adam pleaded, "I wanted to tell you. I tried to tell you all senior year, but I couldn't find a way."

"Why didn't you?" Kevin asked.

"I don't know. It was so long ago. I didn't think it mattered."

"Clearly! It matters now!" Kevin screamed. His voice startled Nancy and Becky, who had kept their eyes to the floor. They looked to Kevin; his face red and flush with anger.

"It was a prank. That's all. It just went wrong."

"You don't do that to friends, Adam. Even when we weren't hanging out together, I always thought you... I always thought you wouldn't..." Kevin stopped. The emotion was too much. He dropped his head to hide the tears.

Francis laughed. Loudly.

"I did what you wanted," Owens said. "You said you'd let me go."

"I did, didn't I?" Francis asked. He raised the gun at Owens and fired. *Bang!*

Owens head snapped back. Blood sprayed across Tanaka's face as the limp body of Carson Owens fell to the ground. Dead.

Becky screamed. Nancy held her ground. She'd seen death before.

"Dammit, Oliver!" Tanaka yelled. "I said, no killing."

"Then you're really not going to like this." Francis fired the gun again.

Bang! Bang!

Tanaka's chest exploded with red. He slammed against the lockers. The look on his face was of shock. He reached to his chest. Felt the blood. He rubbed the holes in his chest. He looked to the smiling face of Francis, waiting for the answer to the question in his head: *Why?*

He grew tired. He lost his willingness to stand up, sliding down along the wall of lockers.  His blood smeared across the locker doors. Francis laughed. He stood over Tanaka, then turned to Adam. "Looks like I stained your old locker, Parker."

Adam glared at Francis, but something caught his eye in the darkness behind him. Down the hallway. A shadow emerged. It was holding a gun.

"What now, Francis?" Adam asked.

"Isn't it obvious? I've revealed your true nature to the people you care about the most. Now they know what you are."

"And what's that?"

Francis stepped fast. He brought his face inches away from Adam's face. He held the heated muzzle to Adam's cheek, burning the skin. Adam flinched. "A monster," he growled.

"You didn't have to kill Owens and Tanaka to show me that."

"I know. I hadn't really planned on Tanaka. Who cares about Owens though? He deserved it. You all do. All you bullies. You all think you're better than everyone else because why? Some stupid notion that you're smarter. Better looking. Able to talk to girls. You don't fool me. You're just as scared as everyone else."

"No shit," Adam shot back. "You act like I got out of bed all those years ago and thought of ways to make your life a living hell."

"Don't tell me it was just high school. I don't want to hear that shit again."

"Fine. How about some truth then? Some real truth," Adam didn't break eye contact. The shadow moved closer, but it needed more time to get behind Francis. "I liked it. All of it. Sure, it's a bit embarrassing now. Having to relive it in front of everyone I care about. But back then? It was fun."

Francis's smile faded. His rage mounting. "Finally. The real Adam Parker emerges."

"I'm so tired of hearing how bad you felt. Boo-hoo. You didn't want to get picked on? Then why didn't you grow a sac and stand up for yourself? You were bullied because you allowed it to happen. Why do you think I never stopped? Because I knew you wouldn't fight back."

"Careful, Parker. I've got the gun."

"Big deal. It's easy to kill Owens. To kill Tanaka. To kill those two cops. Thompson. You didn't care about them."

"Ha! And I care about you?"

"Damn right you do. You did all of this for me. The scavenger hunt. Kidnapping my friend. Meeting here at our special place. You planned all of this from that nut farm in Brookville. I've been on your mind ever since graduation. All you've done is think about me and what you want to do to me."

"And what's that?"

"Why don't you just show me, Same Pants."

Francis's face froze. He stepped back. Raised the gun to Adam's head. Before he could pull the trigger, he dropped to the ground. Tackled by the shadow from the corner of the hallway.

Kenney shoved his knee into the middle of Francis's back, preventing him from moving. Francis was face down. He screamed, but having Kenney's full bodyweight pushing down on him, created an exasperated sigh.

# Chapter 24
## It's Over

The Hilldale High parking lot was now full of Hilldale's finest. Red and blue lights lit up the front of the school. People from the neighboring homes gathered in the parking lot, hoping for a peek at whatever had happened. They were held back by yellow tape, which spanned the entirety of the parking lot.

Adam sat on the front steps of the school. He stared at Francis, who was sitting in the back of a police car. His head was down. Emotionless. A police officer stood guard by the car. Adam's eyes wandered to the back of an ambulance where Kevin sat with Nancy. Nancy continued to adjust the blanket over Kevin's shoulder as he rested his head on her shoulder. They never looked up.

In the distance, Becky stood underneath one of the halogen lamps as her husband, Mark, listened to the story of what had taken place inside the school. He rubbed her back. Supportive. Understanding. She hugged him. They held the embrace.

Adam didn't realize Kenney had taken a seat next to him. "What're you thinking about?"

"That it's over."

"Still some questions though."

"Mine or yours?"

"That was some smart thinking on your part. In there. Distracting him so I could get close enough."

Adam smirked. "I figured you'd say it was reckless."

Kenney held his hand out horizontal and tipped it back and forth like a see-saw. "It's a fine line."

Adam's face cracked with the tiniest of smiles. "How'd you find us?"

"Luck, mainly. Went back to *Lonnie's Tavern*, trying to figure out how Gloria fit into all of this. The girl from the bar."

"The alley was behind Tanaka's restaurant," Adam added.

"You figured that out?"

"Not really. I didn't know Tanaka was working at the *Slammin' Sushi* until we found the first clue there. It wasn't until we got to the final clue at the convenience store that I realized all the stories were about Francis except the Tanaka-Bomb one."

"Tanaka-Bomb?"

"Long story. Short version is I'm an ass."

"I'd still like to know that story, but it can wait. So, you suspected Tanaka, but you didn't know for sure until you saw him tonight."

"Yeah. I knew he had help. There was a lot of moving parts to this thing for one person to handle. Especially one as unhinged as Oliver. I just didn't know who it was."

"I know the connection. About ten minutes ago, I received a phone call from our mutual friend, Sheriff Copeland in Brookville."

"Brookville again? They're all over this."

"No kidding. When I visited the sanitarium, I asked for a list of employees over the last five years. They finally got around to providing it."

"Tanaka worked there."

"In the cafeteria. He must've met Francis at some point. They remember each other. Share a few high school stories. Your name comes up."

"And the rest is history," Adam offered with no joy.

"Something else. Another name. Gloria Hicks."

"The girl from the bar? She worked there?"

"She was a patient. The sanitarium forgot to mention that they actually were missing a patient when I went up there specifically for that reason. I guess I didn't ask the right question. Since it was a woman, they didn't think we were interested in that. Idiots."

"Hicks, Francis and Tanaka all knew each other?" Adam asked.

"I think Hicks and Francis were close. He checks himself out. He's got his plans for you, but she can't leave, so he takes her with him. They come to Hilldale to meet with Tanaka and start planning."

"What was Hicks suffering from?"

"Several things, but mainly she was bi-polar. She was on a slew of medication."

"Medication they couldn't take with them. Or find without bringing too much attention to them. So slowly she starts regressing until... Francis dumps her in the bar?"

Kenney nodded. "We'll get back to that. So, I discover a make-shift gate on the fence behind *Lonnie's* that leads to the *Slammin' Sushi*. Suddenly, I'm in this garden straight out of Japan. Even came with its own cabin."

"Cabin? Where we were held?"

"Seems like it."

"I saw trees and a forest out the window," Adam said, trying to understand.

"You were looking at a monitor. A high-end one from what the forensics team tells me."

Adam cursed quietly under his breath. "I can't believe I missed that."

"You were under some intense pressure, I'm sure," Kenney offered. "Anyway, after discovering that, I showed a picture of Tanaka and Francis to the bartender at the tavern. He recognized them. Said they hung out there often with a girl. Huddled in the corner booth. Talking all hours of the night. I showed him a picture of Hicks. He says she was with them."

"Why didn't he ID her the night you found her?"

"That was my first thought. I almost smacked him, but then he told me he was on vacation that week. He didn't know who the girl was when he got back. Just that we found some girl in the basement."

Adam almost laughed. "C'mon."

Kenney nodded. He didn't believe it either. "This job, Parker. Sometimes, it's as simple as that."

"So, no meds cause Hicks to regress. Francis leaves her in the basement of the bar, knowing that someone will find her. He figures if someone finds her, they'll connect her to him and then his reason for being in Hilldale will be discovered. So, his plan against me is forced into action."

"The other victim. Owens. Who was he in all of this?" Kenney asked.

"Collateral damage. Another bully from the past."

"Jesus. Was high school really that bad back then?"

"Honestly. I don't know."

Kenney paused. This was a new experience for him - The vulnerability of Adam. He didn't know what to say. He took in the scene in front of them, realizing the eyeballs looking in their direction. He spotted Francis in squad car. "It's over now."

"What happens to Francis?"

"He killed five people, including two officers. He's going away for the rest of his life."

"They're going to put him back in the sanitarium," Adam said.

"I know. We'll just have to make sure he stays there."

"He's Brookville's problem now?" Adam asked, half smile on his face.

Kenney laughed. "Yeah. Now it's my turn to give Copeland a hard time about his residents."

Adam's smile faded. He spotted Kevin again, but this time Kevin was staring on him. Watching their conversation. Adam sensed the hatred in his friend's glare.

"You know. I still don't know if Francis would've killed me. I think he just wanted to make the people around me know what type of person I was or am, I guess," Adam said.

"And what's that?"

"A bully. A tormentor. Someone who ruined his life and the lives of anyone in my wake during those four years of school."

"Jesus, Parker. It's just high school. You were teenagers. Everyone does stupid stuff when they're young."

"That's what I kept saying, but... I don't know. Some people can't let it go. They hold onto that baggage and it festers. It shapes the way they behave as adults. How they treat others. Who they blame for their faults. Everything is easy for me to blow off. Why is that? Why am I okay with the death and the mayhem? Why don't psychos like the Scout or Francis scare me? I've never had a meaningful relationship. I purposely keep everyone at a distance. All of these character traits, could they have started in high school? Am I, now, the sum of what I once was?"

Kenney rubbed the back of his neck. "I don't know, Parker. And you're getting a little too philosophical for me right now. What I do know is that your best friend is sitting in that ambulance over there. He's staring at us right now, actually. He looks mad."

"He's mad because he discovered what I am. A lousy friend."

"What're you saying?"

"Nothing. The same thing I always say. Nothing."

Kenney opened his mouth to offer a few more words of encouragement but opted for silence instead. He placed his hand on Adam's shoulder for support, then left him alone on the steps. Kenney sought out his team of officers to go over the most important part of the night - The Coffee Run.

Adam realized he was alone and took the opportunity to sneak away. He noticed that Kevin had returned to the loving embrace of his girlfriend, no longer staring him down. Becky and Mark had moved to the front of their car. They sat on the hood, their backs to the chaos of the parking lot.

Adam wanted to talk to all of them. He wanted to see how they felt, but it didn't feel right. The best and only thing he could do was just leave. And that's what he did as he moved around a few police cars that were parked by the front entrance, lights still flashing. They clearly skidded to a stop and the officers just left them there when they first arrived on scene.

"Hey."

Adam was at the edge of the long driveway leading to the school, his escape route. He spun around to see Kevin standing by the police cars that Adam just passed. He was alone. Blanket off. "Where are you going?"

"Home, I guess. I didn't want to hang around for the news crews to show up," Adam offered.

"Or to talk to us?"

"That, too." Adam closed the distance between them. "Didn't think you'd want to talk about tonight."

"You saved my life."

"I never thought he was going to kill you."

"Maybe, but still. You stopped him."

Adam wanted to stop dancing around the issue. Before he could address it, Kevin spoke. "You know. That night, I was working at the theater. The fire. I remember getting a phone call from my parents about it. I came home early and by then, the tree was no longer burning. They had put it out. I asked my dad what happened, and he didn't know. He said he came to the door and the tree was on fire."

"I don't understand."

Kevin continued, "He knew it was you, Adam. If it was anyone else, my father would've just told me that he fell for the oldest prank in the books. We would've laughed about it.

But he knew you did it. And rather than tell me, worried that I would find out it was you, he kept it to himself."

"Because he knew what would happen."

"He knew we wouldn't be friends anymore. Not after that."

"We're still friends. I'm still your friend."

Kevin grabbed Adam's shirt. He pulled him close. Adam didn't resist. "You son-of-a-bitch! All this time I thought…"

Adam said, "I know. I know."

"We were friends! Dammit! We were friends!"

"We still are."

Kevin pushed him away. Adam stumbled and landed on the pavement. He didn't get up. Kevin stood over him. He jammed his finger at him. "The worst thing is that you would've gone on like it never happened. If Francis didn't show up, I would've never known how you betrayed me all those years ago."

Adam didn't respond. He dropped his head. Shame. Guilt. Kevin backed away. He returned to Nancy. He left Adam laying on the pavement. Alone.

# Chapter 25
## Weeks Later

The moving truck was in Adam's driveway all morning. The movers were in and out of the house, filling up the truck with everything not nailed down inside. Adam spent most of the morning leaning on his car, watching the movers go about their business. He'd occasionally glance in the direction of Kevin's house, but knew there was never any hope of the front door opening.

It had been weeks since the incident at the school. That was the last time Kevin and Adam spoke. Adam kept his distance. If he saw Kevin outside, he stayed indoors. If he spotted Kevin working at the movie theater, Adam would find something else to do. Kevin returned to his old job. A sign that Adam took as his best friend was moving on from the life of being a detective. A few times, Adam bumped into Nancy, but the conversations were limited to casual greetings and nothing more.

Even his contact with Becky was limited. Adam already knew she was quitting the agency. She brought it up to him the day after the incident, but Adam stopped her. He told her he understood, and everything would be fine. And that was the last time they spoke about it.

For right now, he was moving out. The house was too big for him and his mother could use the extra money. After the events at the school, Adam called his mother at her retirement village in Florida to tell her it was time. He didn't want to hang around for the sale, so he moved his stuff out. His mother's stuff, which was filling up the truck fast, was being sent to Florida for her to do with what she wanted.

"Leaving again?" It was Becky. She called from her porch.

Adam waved and jogged over to her. "Hey."

"One of the PTO Moms said she heard this house was on the market. I didn't want to believe her."

"And yet here we are," Adam confirmed the rumor.

"Seriously? You're leaving us."

"Contrary to your expectations and those expectations of many others, I am only leaving the neighborhood. The house is too big for just me."

"You're staying in Hilldale?"

"Downtown. I found an apartment."

"Well, that's something."

"It is. How's Mark? He still hate me?"

"Off and on. Now, that I've called it a career. He's happy."

"Are you?"

She shrugged. "I suppose. I miss it. But I need to be present for my family."

"Sure. I get that."

They paused. It was as awkward as they hoped it wouldn't be.

Becky broke the silence first. "You okay?"

It was Adam's turn to shrug. "We stopped him. We saved the day again...sort of. But at what cost. My friendships. My reputation."

"To be fair, your reputation wasn't that great."

He laughed. "This is true."

"And I'm still your friend."

"Even after what you learned about me?"

She scoffed. "I knew what type of person you were, Adam Parker. Sure, you have checkered past of being an asshole, but it's just that. The past. Let it go."

"I'm trying. But..." He looked to Kevin's house, not realizing he was doing it. He bowed his head.

"He'll come around. Just give him time."

The Simpson front door opened. Henry, Kevin's father, ambled out. He spotted the moving truck and then Adam. He waved.

"Excuse me," Adam said as he jogged across the street to see Mr. Simpson. After a friendly return wave and an exchange of pleasantries:

"I can't believe you're leaving us."

"Just the neighborhood. I'll be downtown."

Henry smiled. "Excellent. It'll give me a reason to go down there."

"Mr. Simpson, I wanted to talk to you about something."

"The tree?"

"Kevin told you. I figured he would."

Henry placed his hand on Adam's shoulder. "I'll tell you what I told him. Teenagers are stupid. Why would you be any different?"

Adam smiled. "I nearly caused a major disaster though."

"You lit a bag of dog poop on fire. Honestly, I should've known better than to stomp on it. And kicking it in the tree, well that was just hilarious." He laughed.

"I can't believe you're okay with it."

"Well, when it first happened, I wasn't. But I saw you behind the car. You really shouldn't hide behind a window. I saw your face. Your friend was laughing his ass off, but you were scared. Nervous. Afraid. When I saw that, I knew you didn't know what would happen. I knew you made a stupid decision and I didn't blame you. I've never blamed you."

Adam smirked. "Thanks, Mr. Simpson."

"Give Kevin some time. He'll come around."

"Is he here?" Adam asked.

"No. He left early today. Said he had to meet someone. Probably his new girlfriend. She's scary."

"She sure is."

They shared a laugh.

* * *

Kevin walked right down the middle of the hallway, behind the orderly, as instructed. He was careful to avoid eye contact with the more expressive people residing the wing. Although, he was assured that he was in no danger, Kevin was careful nonetheless. He didn't think he'd gain access, but when the staff relayed his name to the patient, approval was quickly given.

After numerous pages of paperwork that required his signature, Kevin was led up a stairwell and through a locked cage that provided access to the second-floor hallway. He passed several rooms of patients. Some crying. Some screaming. Some sitting perfectly still. One woman called out to him by name, but he figured his orderly escort had the same name. He hoped, at least.

He was led to Room 23, where a patient stood with his back to the doorway. He stood at a window, overlooking a large field of grass, which was surrounded by a newly installed security fence. Oliver Francis turned to greet Kevin with a smile. His hair no longer long and stringy, but newly shorn.

"Ah, Simpson. I was hoping you'd visit me."

"You were?"

Francis looked to the orderly. "We're okay here, Steve. Thanks."

Steve nodded and remained outside the room.

Kevin did a double-take at the name. *Did that patient really know his name?* He mentally wiped that concern from his mind. He confessed, "Honestly, I don't know why I came."

"Because we're not done."

"It was something you said to me at the cabin. Well, actually, it wasn't a cabin now, was it?"

"Jeff's idea. He had dabbled with some audio-visual technology in college and he thought it would be a good idea to utilize it. To keep all the players close together." Francis looked out the window. "I wonder where Jeff is. I thought he'd visit me by now."

"You killed him. Remember? You shot him in the chest."

Francis snapped his fingers as if remembering, "Yes. I did. Didn't I?"

"Anyway, while I was being held captive, you said that after high school we either evolve into better or worse versions of ourselves."

"I may have said that. I mean, that sounds like me."

"Why do you assume Adam was worse?"

Francis paused. "What's that?"

"You just assumed that Adam grew up to become worse than he was when he was bullying you in school. Why?"

"Because, your friend is evil. The devil incarnate. He tormented me, not only for those four years of high school, but for the years after."

"He continued to bully you?"

"Not him. People like him. They would tease me. Laugh at me. Make fun of me. Make me do things I didn't want to do."

Kevin stepped closer. "But that didn't happen to me. After high school, I went to college and made friends. Good friends. I met people who liked the things I liked. The same movies and TV shows. I have deep, long-lasting friendships to this day."

"Your point?"

"Adam was a bully to you. That'll never change but he left your life after his senior year of school. You don't know what type of person he became."

"And you do?"

"Better than you, I think."

"Tell me, Simpson. Does he make fun of you? Does he crack jokes at your behalf? Does he take your friendship for granted? We already know he's lied to you. Why would you think he hasn't lied to you about anything else?"

Kevin was silent. He couldn't answer the questions.

"You see, Simpson. You have no idea what type of person Parker has become," Francis stepped closer. "I've given you a gift. I shined a light on your friend and now you cannot ignore his lies. You cannot ignore the jokes. You're a free man. Free to rid yourself of Adam Parker and move on with your life. People like Parker like to be alone. They don't want friends. They don't need human connections."

"You're starting to sound like you're envious of that." Kevin cut him off.

"Oh, I am! If I didn't allow myself to have feelings, I would've never brought Gloria with us. Her deterioration forced my hand. And Jeff, well he wasn't exactly the greatest partner. I lacked what Adam already had, the innate design to be alone."

Kevin looked around the room. "Well, you've got your wish."

Francis smiled. "Exactly." He turned his back on Kevin and walked to the window. He pushed aside the curtain and looked at the other patients in the field below. "I'll be seeing you soon, Kevin."

Kevin backed out of the room, regretting his decision for the visit.

* * *

The apartment had a bed. It had a desk. It had a TV. And it had countless boxes of Adam's stuff piled high all around. Adam carried everything he owned up the flight of stairs in one afternoon and then spent the night passed out on a mattress on the floor as the metal bed frame leaned against the wall. Adam was too tired to put his bed together.

The next morning, he took the stairs down to the street and several steps later, found himself inside *Crepes and Coffee* ordering just what the name on the sign said. He filled up his coffee-to-go cup and headed back to his apartment building.

A faded *"For Lease"* sign sat in the window of what used to be the *Slammin' Sushi* restaurant. Adam felt bad for Tanaka's uncle. He shouldn't have to suffer the sins of the nephew, especially one they lost so young.

At the bottom of his apartment building, there was a storefront. Adam turned the key in door of the storefront and entered. A sign hung on the inside of the door. He flipped it around from *Closed* to *Open.* The larger, hand painted sign on the giant window read: *The Parker Detective Agency.*

There was a desk in the back. A phone on the desk. Rotary dial because he found it in a storage room and in an effort to save money, he didn't want to buy a new one. Besides, he liked the retro feel for it. The money that would've bought a new phone went towards a laptop, which sat atop the desk. Adam pulled it open as he took a seat.

He sipped his coffee and looked out the front window at the people walking along the sidewalk. He was amidst Kevin's vision. A legit detective agency, only Kevin and Becky were no longer part of the team. He was alone, but finally accepting of his calling.

*Ring! Ring!* The phone rang.

Adam thought of their earlier cases. When they were three pre-teens looking to be local heroes. The wooden sign that hung on the garage door. The ridiculous go-kart that Kevin always drove around town. Adam smiled at the thought of the first time they met Becky, as she charged from her back porch asking them to find out if her boyfriend was cheating on her.

Ring! Ring!

Adam remembered four months ago. His desperation in that diner. Kevin coming to his aide. The joy in his face as they investigated the hardware store burglary. Adam initially fought the feeling that rose in his belly during the Scout case. The sense of purpose he had been looking for when he moved out of Hilldale. He had found it again. In his home town. Alongside his best friend.

Ring! Ring!

Adam was a damn good detective. His mother always said that it was in his DNA, from a father he never knew. Adam had only seen his Dad in photos, but he couldn't help but feel his presence when he worked a case. The deductions, the connections, even the calm feeling Adam felt during tension-filled times came from somewhere.

From those kid detective days to these messy adult times, Adam arrived at the one thing that gave him comfort. His calling. The agency. He finally accepted his path. A path that his best friend pushed him to be on. A best friend who begged him to accept his fate. A best friend that was no longer by his side. Adam was alone now on this path. It wasn't what he wanted at first, but now, there was nothing else he wanted to be:

Adam Parker: P.I.

"Dammit. That's dumb." He said out loud.

He didn't like that title. As soon as he thought of it, he hated it and he hated the fact that he thought of it. He didn't want to start wearing fedoras and suits. For some reason those images popped into his head. Would he start talking like people in classic movies? Would he start telling people 'here's looking at you"? Would give weird nicknames to people like 'kid' or 'doll'?

Adam Parker: Not a P.I., but something like it without the lame stuff.

Ring! Ring!

He answered the phone.

THE END

# A Word from the Author

I started this book two years ago, but I also started a graduate school program at the same time. Not the brightest idea, so this second book took a bit longer than anticipated. Nevertheless, I was able to earn my master's degree in Interactive Media from Quinnipiac University and focus on the continuing story of Adam Parker and his struggle with being an adult.

I wanted to explore the idea of perspective with this story. We often view ourselves in a way that runs contrary to another's perspective. When I was a younger man, I may have found something funny while another person would see me as being rude. Even now, my actions and words are perceived a different way than how I view them and understanding that concept is the best way to becoming a better person.

My favorite exchange in the book is when Adam surmises: "It was high school. Who didn't get bullied?" and Becky replies "Bullies." Exactly.

Thank you to my wife, Jody, who provided the cover art for this book. Much of this book is inspired by my enjoyment of the Encyclopedia Brown stories from my youth and they're still going strong today, so thank you to Mr. Sobol for providing a great a character to use as a backboard for Adam Parker.

Adam, Kevin and Becky are not based on any one person, but a collection of traits and ideas I've come across throughout my life. There are pieces of me in all three characters. Kevin's love for movies, Adam's sarcastic, often infuriating sense of humor and Becky's sense to be true top herself and what she loves to name a few. Thank you to all who inspire these characters.

And thank you, the reader, for coming along on another Adam Parker adventure. I have plans for Mr. Parker and friends, so perhaps we will all meet again in a future story.

# About the Author

Michael is a member of the Writer's Guild of America. He was nominated for a 2017 WGA Award for Outstanding Writing in New Media for the digital short – Life Ends @ 30. He's the creator of the web series, The Puzzle Maker's Son and Scenes from the Movies. His screenplay, Kiddo, was a quarterfinalist for the 2015 Nicholl Fellowship and is currently being shopped to studios. He currently resides in Connecticut with his wife, three children, four dogs and two bunnies.

# Connect with the Author

Follow Michael on Twitter: @mdfield
Personal Website: www.michaeldfield.com

Made in the USA
Middletown, DE
28 February 2019